# THE LOCATORS

## ADVENTURE IN SOUTH AMERICA

WRITTEN BY KYLE BAUER

CONCEPT BY COLLEEN CONNER

ILLUSTRATED BY WESLEY JONES

Esri Press
REDLANDS | CALIFORNIA

# FOR CAMERON AND BROOKLYN

Esri Press, 380 New York Street, Redlands, California 92373-8100
Copyright © 2021 Esri
All rights reserved.
Printed in the United States of America
25 24 23 22 21       2 3 4 5 6 7 8 9 10

ISBN: 9781589484986
Library of Congress Control Number: 2021934420

For purchasing and distribution options (both domestic and international), please visit esripress.esri.com.

# CONTENTS

# MISSIONS

*Over the course of their adventure, Lucy, Oliver, and Moe the Parrot will need your help navigating South America! Put your skills to the test by working through Missions.*

**WHEN YOU SEE THIS BEAUTIFUL FACE, IT'S MISSION TIME!**

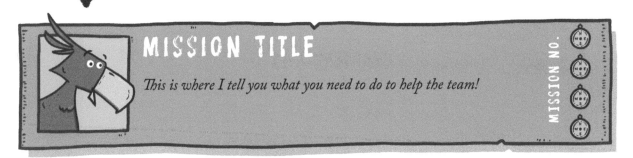

## MISSION TITLE

*This is where I tell you what you need to do to help the team!*

MISSION NO.

**THE NUMBER OF COMPASSES INDICATES THE MISSION'S DIFFICULTY. THIS ONE HAS ALL FOUR – YIKES!**

# CONTINUE EXPLORING ONLINE

*All the mission pages, as well as additional activities and resources for how to continue your mapping adventure, can be discovered online at:*

**go.esri.com/locators**

## LUCY

## ADVANCED SKILLS

*Mountaineering*
*Swimming*
*Orienteering*

## LOCATOR MEMBER ID 12705118608

*Lucy is a natural leader. Always with a map in hand, she jumps at the chance to solve problems. She loves finding ways for humans and animals to live in harmony.*

# OLIVER

## ADVANCED SKILLS

*Flying*
*Mechanics*
*Hot Dog Eating*

## LOCATOR MEMBER ID 12795105516

*Oliver is exceptionally mechanical. His dream is to become a pilot,*
*flying missions to any part of the planet that needs his help.*

MOE

## ADVANCED SKILLS

*Flying*
*Linguistics*
*Wit*

## LOCATOR MEMBER ID

*Moe is a parrot, and Oliver is his best friend. Moe complains
a lot, but deep down he is a kind bird. Helping Oliver and
Lucy solve problems is his favorite thing.*

# YOUR NAME

## ADVANCED SKILLS

1.

2.

3.

## WRITE A COUPLE OF SENTENCES ABOUT YOU

## LOCATOR MEMBER ID

*You will earn your member ID by the end of the book!*

# PART 1

AMAZON

"Wow, I can't believe this view," Lucy said, eyes glued to the small plane's window as thousands of trees passed below. It was the Amazon rain forest, the largest rain forest in the world. She, her friend Oliver, and her parrot, Moe, had flown far to reach this amazing biome in South America. It was even greener than she'd imagined. Best. Summer. Vacation. Ever!

They didn't come to sight-see, however. Lucy and Oliver's teacher, Professor Meridian, had given them their first mission as Locators. The Locators were a group of kids who solved problems in the world using maps, technology, and spatial thinking.

Lucy, Oliver, and Moe had been recruited by Professor Meridian to join her special school and the Locators, and now they were finally going on a mission. Lucy was *so* ready to prove to her professor that she could count on Lucy and her team.

Their first mission was to find and protect one of the rain forest's most endangered species, the jaguar. Deforestation threatened jaguars across the Amazon, and Professor Meridian had received an alert that there'd been an increase in jaguar sightings near towns recently. She'd deployed the Locators to find out what was happening, and Lucy wasn't about to let her down.

Oliver seemed…less enthusiastic. Ever since they'd reached the Amazon, he'd been nervously checking the plane's autopilot system and muttering to himself. Usually, Oliver knew everything there was to know about computers and technology, so this was a worrying sign.

"What's wrong, Oliver?" Lucy asked.

"Um, nothing! Nothing at all. We should arrive any minute."

Moe popped up from the back seat in a puff of feathers. "Yeah, right! We're flying in circles."

"We are?" Lucy said. With only forest in every direction, it was hard to tell.

"I'm a bird, I know a thing or two about flying. If I say we're lost, it means WE'RE LOST!"

Trying to keep calm, Lucy grabbed her tablet from her backpack and pulled up the map the professor had given them. It showed the route from their hometown to their destination. But without more information, she couldn't tell where the plane was.

"I don't get it. We should be close," Oliver said. "The landing strip is only a tiny distance away on the map. I overrode the autopilot to make the plane circle around, thinking we would see it eventually, but…"

Lucy realized the problem. Nothing was wrong with the map—Oliver just wasn't reading it right. Although the Amazon on the map didn't look big, that was because of the map's scale. The "tiny distance" Oliver saw on the map represented *hundreds* of miles in the real world. Who knew how far away they were?

"*SQUAWK!*" Moe fluttered onto Lucy's shoulder and pointed to the fuel gauge with his wings. "You better figure out where we need to go soon or else we'll run out of gas."

As soon as he said it, the gauge started to blink—it was almost empty! The plane had flown in circles for too long. Now they probably wouldn't have enough fuel even if they *did* know where to go.

"This is bad," Oliver said, eyes wide.

"What can we do?" Lucy asked. She searched the vast rain forest below.

Her eyes settled on a clearing near a river. "There," she said, pointing. "Do you think we can land there?"

"The autopilot system isn't designed to land without a runway."

"We're not going to find a runway in time. It's either there or in the trees," Lucy said. She *really* hoped it wouldn't be in the trees. "I know you can do it."

Oliver gulped. He flipped some switches and changed some settings. "OK, I'll try. But it's going to be bumpy. Everyone, buckle up."

"See, that was easy," Lucy said as she climbed out of the cockpit. They'd managed to land, but one glance at the plane and she knew it was wrecked.

"Oh no," Oliver groaned, "our equipment is ruined. We're doomed!" He rummaged around inside the plane before coming out with the phone Professor Meridian had given them. "Even the phone is busted."

Lucy frowned at Oliver's dramatics, then took stock of the surroundings: dense foliage and underbrush. Birds sang from the treetops (Moe squawked back). In the distance loomed a single, jagged peak.

"Doomed!" Oliver fell to his knees. "We have no clue where we are and there's jungle for miles in every direction."

"*SQUAWK*," Moe said. "You humans may be doomed, but for me this is a hot vacation spot."

"Everyone keep calm." Lucy pressed a button on her tablet. "We'll ask Professor Meridian for help on this instead." The tablet crackled to life. Luckily, the professor had modified it before their mission to receive a signal even in the most remote areas.

Professor Meridian appeared on-screen. Each wall of her office had

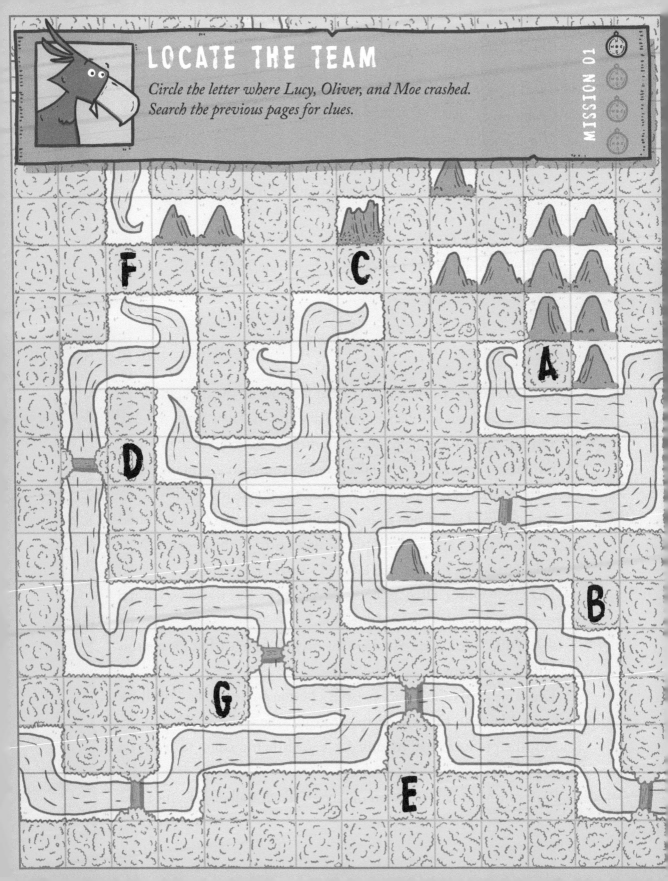

# LOCATE THE TEAM

*Circle the letter where Lucy, Oliver, and Moe crashed.*
*Search the previous pages for clues.*

a monitor with a high-tech map. On her desk, though, was an old-fashioned globe.

Lucy explained the situation.

"Aha, it's quite the pickle you've gotten yourselves into, my intrepid students," the professor said. She placed a hand under her chin, tapping it with one finger as she considered them.

"I'm sorry I wrecked the plane, Professor," Oliver said.

"Don't worry—these things happen when you're on an adventure, believe me. Now, I'm sending you a map of the northern Amazon basin. Investigate your surroundings and see if you can determine your location on the map."

# CHAPTER 2

"I think I found where we are," Lucy said after comparing the map to their surroundings. "It looks like we're close to the mountain called Pico da Neblina."

"Very good. That means you've crashed only 200 miles from your destination." The professor made it sound like a good thing, but 200 miles was a *long* way. "Tell me, in which cardinal direction does the mountain lie?"

Lucy pulled out her trusty compass. The dial indicated that Pico da Neblina was to the north.

"Superb!" the professor said. "You're only a few miles from a camp of soil researchers. One of them is a former Locator member."

"So there'll be a helicopter there to take us where we need to go?" Oliver looked ready to jump for joy. He preferred working on a computer to hiking through the jungle.

"Nope," Professor Meridian said. Oliver's face fell. "But they can help you get there in other ways. Then you'll be able to investigate what's threatening jaguars in the Amazon."

Lucy was eager to get going. This was her first chance to study animals up close. She wondered what a jaguar looked like in the wild, creeping through underbrush, stalking its prey. She tugged Oliver in the direction to leave, only to remember she didn't know the way yet.

"Professor," she said to the tablet, "can you add the camp's location to the map?"

"Already done," Professor Meridian said. On the tablet, the map zoomed in and showed the area in more detail. "It's up to you to plot your route."

# LOCATE THE SHORTEST ROUTE

*Draw the shortest path from the crash to the camp. Avoid rivers and mountains, and do not move diagonally. There are several routes, so think about why yours is the shortest.*

CRASH

CAMP

"I think my backpack is going to crush me," Oliver said, huffing under the weight. It *did* look a little stuffed to Lucy. But after the team had determined they needed to walk east and then south to reach the camp, they'd loaded up on the supplies they could salvage from the plane: food, water, tents, and equipment. The entire trip would span about 60 miles, which meant they needed as much as they could carry.

Unfortunately, the dense Amazon forest impeded their progress at every step. Lucy, leading the way, slashed a path through thick vines and tangled brush with a machete. It rained the whole time. Although the trees formed a canopy above them, they were quickly soaked to the bone.

"*SQUAWK!*" Moe ruffled his feathers to shake off the water. "They don't call it the *rain* forest for nothing."

"I should've packed an umbrella," Oliver said as he tried to wipe his glasses dry with his shirt. It was no use.

As Lucy pushed through the next layer of underbrush, she suddenly stopped. Clinging to a tree branch high above them was a medium-size furred creature with long arms and claws. It crawled extremely slowly along the branch, not slipping despite the rain.

"A sloth," Lucy whispered, trying to keep her excitement contained so she didn't spook the animal. She recognized it from their biology class. This was the best trip ever!

Oliver stopped beside her. "It moves so slowly. Doesn't it have to worry about predators?"

"It's high in the trees. Not much can reach it." Lucy pulled her notebook from class out of her bag and shielded it from the rain. "Let's see,

the brown-throated sloth… Its primary natural predators are harpy eagles and…jaguars."

Oliver gulped and glanced over his shoulder nervously. "Do you think a jaguar's around right now?"

"Probably not the best time to find out," Lucy said, taking one last look at the sloth. "Come on, let's go."

"We made it," Oliver shouted, whooping in joy as they came to a stop. After several days of rugged hiking, they'd finally reached the camp where a group of scientists were studying the rain forest's soil. The camp was no more than a few tents in the jungle, but after a long trek through wilderness, *anything* was welcome.

One of the researchers approached them, a tall, dark-haired woman who introduced herself as Dr. Carvalho. "You must be Lucy, Oliver, and Moe. It's nice to meet you. Your professor, Dr. Meridian, is my former teacher," she said. "She called me by radio to explain the situation. So, you want to find the jaguars? Then you have a long way yet to go."

After their long journey to get to camp, that was the *last* thing Lucy wanted to hear. How was the Amazon so big? She was already exhausted, and she knew the others were, too.

"Why can't we research jaguars here?" Oliver asked, eyeing the camp's computer equipment longingly. "We're in the Amazon, right? Do jaguars only appear in certain parts?"

"Jaguars live all over the Amazon," Dr. Carvalho said. "But if you want to find out what's threatening them, you'll have to go to where people live."

They spent the night in camp and got to watch the researchers work. Many went on expeditions into the rain forest, while others came back with samples of dirt. They examined the tiny containers of soil with microscopes. One of the researchers explained it was important to monitor soil quality in the Amazon because frequent rains washed away nutrients necessary for plant growth, a process known as leaching.

The next day, the Locators embarked on a motorboat down the Amazon River. Dr. Carvalho helped them navigate the twisting, narrow waterway. They saw small crocodiles—called caimans—lounging on the banks.

"At least we don't have to walk," Oliver said as he tinkered with their busted phone. The Amazon River was one of the longest rivers in the world at 4,000 miles. Walking it would take a *long* time.

"Or fly," Moe added.

"When we arrive," Lucy said, "how will we find a jaguar?"

"That's a good question," Dr. Carvalho said. "Jaguars are solitary creatures that are great at stalking prey. In short, they don't like to be seen. Your best bet is to stake out near a jaguar's preferred habitat."

This mission was turning out to be a lot more difficult than Lucy had thought it would be. But she couldn't let herself get discouraged—being part of the Locators meant more than anything to her. Re-energized, Lucy used her tablet to pull up a map of their destination: the Brazilian state of Roraima, where Professor Meridian believed jaguars were in danger. The **scale bar** told her the area was hundreds of miles wide.

"I can't believe the professor didn't tell us where the jaguars' habitat is," Lucy said.

Moe squawked. "I sure can. That professor's always trying to test you kids. I'm glad bird school's way easier than people school."

"Is 'bird school' even a thing?" Oliver asked.

"Of course. Where do you think I learned to talk?" Moe said.

"You can narrow down the area if you know the places jaguars like best," Dr. Carvalho said. "They're fond of dense forest because they like to hide in the brush. They love to swim, so they hang around areas with lots of water. However, they don't particularly enjoy highlands or mountainous areas."

Lucy examined the map. Based on the clues Dr. Carvalho gave, she tried to think of where a jaguar would most want to live…

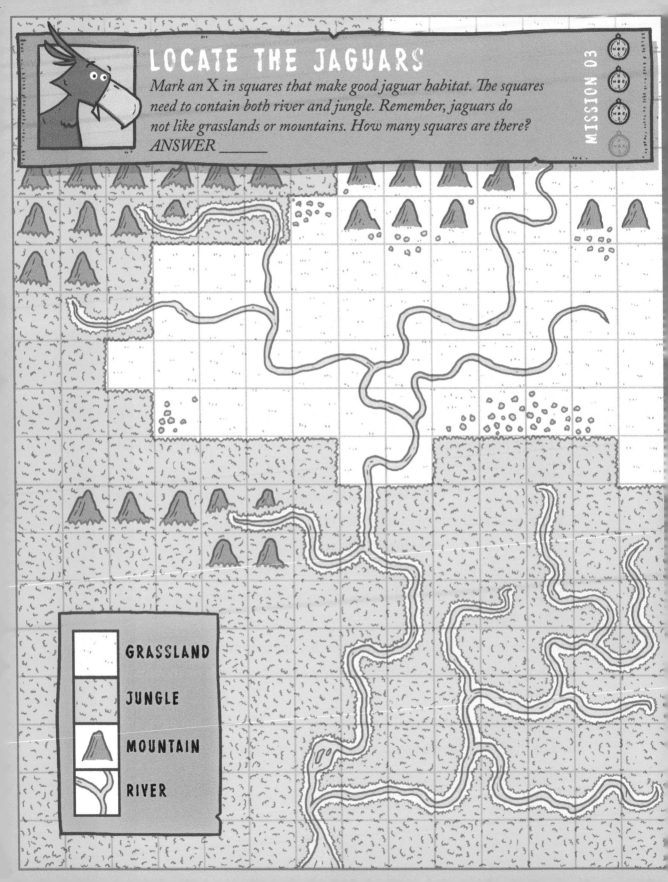

# LOCATE THE JAGUARS

*Mark an X in squares that make good jaguar habitat. The squares need to contain both river and jungle. Remember, jaguars do not like grasslands or mountains. How many squares are there?*
ANSWER _____

GRASSLAND

JUNGLE

MOUNTAIN

RIVER

"I think we're here," Lucy said, glancing around. Dr. Carvalho navigated the motorboat up the river and to the area of Roraima that Lucy had marked on the map. They'd decided the best place to look for jaguars would be the marshy southern part of the state. Thankfully, the boat traveled way faster than walking, so it had only taken them a few hours even though they had a lot of ground to cover.

They disembarked on the eastern bank. They saw the same dense forest as before, but the ground was swampier.

Dr. Carvalho turned the boat around in the river. "My apologies, friends, but I can't accompany you all the way. I have my own research, after all."

"We understand. Thank you for all your help," Oliver said.

"I wish you the best of luck," Dr. Carvalho called as the boat puttered out of sight.

Neither Oliver nor Moe seemed too thrilled to plunge back into the jungle after the relatively breezy boat trip. "Look on the bright side," Lucy told them. "We'll finally see a jaguar!"

"*SQUAWK!* Do jaguars eat parrots?"

"Or people?" added a wary Oliver.

Despite their complaints, Lucy led them onward. They didn't go far before they encountered something surprising: a long clearing in the middle of the forest. Unlike the riverbank clearing they used to land their plane, this clearing didn't look natural. The trees had been cut down, and recently.

"This doesn't seem right." Oliver frowned.

Farther down the clearing, Lucy noticed a simple dirt road. Along the

# JAGUAR

3RD LARGEST MEMBER OF THE BIG CAT FAMILY

WEIGHT: 100-250 POUNDS

NEAR THREATENED: POPULATION DECREASING

road were fences, cattle, and even houses. It no longer felt like they were in the Amazon rain forest.

"Did they cut down the forest to build farms?" Lucy asked.

"I wonder if this is the threat to the jaguars Professor Meridian warned us about," Oliver said, looking sad. "There have been more sightings of jaguars because they lost their habitat here."

It seemed possible. To make sure, Lucy called the professor.

"Astute observation, students," the professor said. "Indeed, the biggest threat to jaguars today is habitat loss, often in the form of deforestation. Without the forest, there's nowhere for jaguars to hunt prey. Worse yet, cattle ranches are often built in deforested areas. While a herd of cows might look like a jaguar all-you-can-eat buffet, ranchers will do anything to stop jaguars from munching on their **livestock**."

Lucy thought that sounded pretty dangerous for the jaguars. "Our map didn't show any of this," Lucy said, frowning.

"It's difficult to show deforestation on a map for two reasons," the professor said. "First, deforestation often happens in small pieces, making it hard to see on maps that show a large area. Also, deforestation changes all the time, so information that's even a few years old might be out of date."

"But if we can't map it," Oliver said, "how will we know where jaguars are threatened?"

Professor Meridian stroked her chin and went "hmm." Finally, she snapped her fingers. "I've got it! Moe, we'll need your help."

Moe hopped onto Lucy's shoulder and preened proudly. "You can count on me. What's the mission, boss?"

"I need you to fly above the area and draw what you see. Many maps are created using photographs taken from planes—what we call aerial imagery. We don't have a plane, but a bird's-eye view is close enough. You can use Moe's map to find the deforestation."

With his wing, Moe saluted. Although he was a bit of a jokester, when he was needed, there was nobody (or no bird) more dependable. Lucy and Oliver watched him shoot off into the sky. Not long after, he returned.

"Here you go, one map, just the way you ordered. Not bad for a bird, right?"

"Thanks, Moe," said Lucy. "Now let's find out where the deforestation is."

# LOCATE THE DEFORESTATION

1. Mark an X on squares that are completely jungle. These are
   fully intact jungle squares.
2. There are several clusters of intact jungle squares. Outline the
   largest cluster.

JUNGLE

CLEARED AREA

ROAD

After looking over the map for a few minutes, Oliver said, "The deforestation must be those weird blocky areas around those lines, right?"

"Those lines are roads," Moe explained. "Pretty good likeness, if I do say so myself."

"Why do you think the deforestation is around the roads, Oliver?" Lucy asked.

"Forests don't grow in rectangular patterns like that. Those patterns have to have been made by people. And if the lines really are roads, then it makes even more sense. People can use the roads to go deeper into the forest to cut down trees."

Lucy was impressed that Oliver was able to figure it out so quickly. But they still had a lot left to do. "Even if we know where deforestation is," Lucy said, "what can we do about it?" She hated feeling helpless. Professor Meridian had given them an impossible mission.

Before Oliver could respond, Moe started flapping his wings and squawking. "Hate to break it to you guys, but we got company!"

Hidden along the outskirts of the jungle was a large, spotted cat. Lucy recognized it immediately: a jaguar. It stalked through the underbrush without making a single sound. Oliver and Moe hid behind a nearby fence, but Lucy was mesmerized as it crept closer to one of the ranches. She saw exactly what it was headed for: a lone bull that grazed along the ranch's pasture. The bull flicked its tail and chewed, blissfully unaware of what lurked behind it.

Lucy waited for the powerful cat to pounce, but right before it did, Oliver shouted, "Watch out!"

The bull looked up with a jolt. As soon as it saw the jaguar lying in wait, it sprinted away with a panicked "moo." The jaguar dashed in pursuit. Prey and predator ran circles around the empty meadow, where there was no cover for the jaguar to hide. Lucy realized the problem even before the door to the ranch house flew open and three very angry farmers barged out with hoes and pitchforks.

The jaguar immediately forgot about the bull. It was outnumbered and in trouble. Like a flash, the jaguar scampered back into the forest without a single ounce of food to show for its effort.

The farmers scowled at where the jaguar had disappeared, muttered something among themselves, and then went back inside the house. The spooked bull returned to grazing.

It took a long time for Lucy to calm down. Oliver and Moe jabbered breathlessly about how big the jaguar was and how fast it ran, but Lucy barely paid them any attention.

The tablet, still clutched in her hand, buzzed with static. They were still in a call with the professor. She said, "I believe you now know a major reason why habitat loss is such a problem for jaguars."

"How do we stop it?" Lucy asked.

"What if we planted more trees?" Oliver said. "If the forest was cut down, it can be grown back, right?"

"But people already live here now," Lucy said, shaking her head.

Moe landed on her shoulder and put up his wings like boxing gloves. "*SQUAWK!* I say boot 'em out."

"We can't do that. And even if we did, don't you remember what the scientists at Dr. Carvalho's camp said? The soil in the Amazon has few nutrients because the rain leached them away. It'll be hard to grow the forest back."

"Then let's move the jaguars somewhere else," Oliver said.

"That won't work, either," Lucy said. She took out her notes on jaguars.

"Jaguars are territorial and solitary. If we move a jaguar where another already lives, they'll probably fight. And if we move a jaguar where no other jaguars live, it might be because it's not a good habitat for them."

They kept offering suggestions, but none that seemed likely to work. Lucy loved brainstorming, but she was starting to get frustrated. If only she could come up with a solution that worked for both the jaguars *and* the ranchers.

"Maybe," said Oliver, after a lot of thinking, "rather than relocate people or jaguars, we find a way for them to live together?"

"Now you're thinking, Oliver," said the professor. "Jaguars have wide hunting grounds that cover a lot of area, but deforestation occurs in a fish-bones pattern that leaves lots of little patches of forest separated by farms and ranches. The jaguars keep intruding in part because there's no other way to move between the fragments of rain forest in their territory."

Lucy snapped her fingers. "Aha, so if we create pathways between the forest fragments, the jaguars won't have as much reason to go to the ranches."

"Stupendous deduction. In fact, a similar strategy has been applied to connect fragmented cougar habitat in California. There, conservationists are designing bridges to go over freeways so cougars can cross safely. They're called habitat corridors."

"Uh, it might be hard to build a bridge over a cattle ranch," Oliver said.

"A habitat corridor need not be so grandiose," Professor Meridian said. "Any safe strip of terrain might work. River passages, abandoned plots of land, or farms without livestock…all could be a jaguar corridor."

"If we only have to protect a few corridors, it'll make it a lot easier to help jaguars," Lucy said.

"Also, if it's only a narrow corridor," Oliver said, "maybe we can plant just a few trees without using up all the soil's nutrients. That'd give the jaguar even more cover, right?"

Professor Meridian gave them a thumbs-up. "I'm so proud of my astute students. You've really got the right idea." She fiddled with some of her mapmaking equipment. "I'm sending a map of the area. This map includes information about deforestation that I created based on the aerial imagery Moe drew earlier. It also has a bunch of information about farms, roads, and rivers. Use it to find as many potential corridor locations as possible."

With that, she was gone and the screen of the tablet changed to show a new map of the area. The Locators were on the job!

# LOCATE POSSIBLE CORRIDORS

Connect the separated jungles by drawing paths between them that create corridors. The paths can only be drawn through abandoned farms and rivers. Each path can go through a maximum of three triangles.

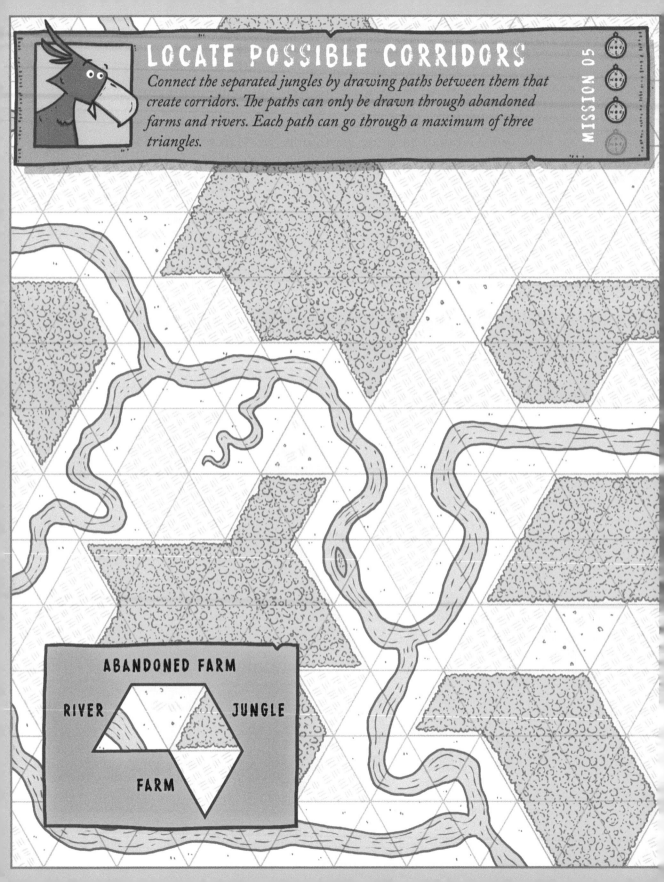

ABANDONED FARM

RIVER    JUNGLE

FARM

With Oliver's help, and even the occasional contribution from Moe, Lucy was able to pick out a large number of places that might make good corridors for jaguars. Without delay, they hiked up and down the area to investigate the potential corridors.

"You're not going to complain about all the walking, Oliver?" Lucy asked as they reached the first location.

"Complain? Me? Never," Oliver said.

"That'll be the day," Moe said, conveniently ignoring that he had complained a lot himself.

It took several days, but they managed to scout every location they chose. Some of the potential corridor locations were no good—there were too many people nearby or the landowners didn't want to help—but most of the locations seemed great. Some farmers were even willing to lend part of their land for a fair price, especially if it would keep the jaguars away from their cattle. Other areas were abandoned and only needed a few more trees to provide perfect cover for a stalking jaguar.

Relieved and excited that her team had managed to complete their first field mission, Lucy sent Professor Meridian a list of the possible corridors.

"I'll contact the necessary authorities to work on renting or purchasing the land," the professor said. "We'll chalk the cost down to 'research expenses,' now, won't we?" She winked and Lucy laughed. Their school often gave out big scholarships for research. "Now you can spend the rest of your time studying the jaguar in its natural habitat."

For the next week, they searched for the elusive jaguar in the wild, but had little luck. Then, on the day before they were set to leave, while she and Oliver were walking along a river, they saw one: a jaguar. It watched them from the other side of the bank, flicking its tail patiently.

Lucy fumbled with her backpack to grab her notes but stopped when she saw something else moving near the jaguar. No, two somethings—jaguar cubs. The cubs, as small as regular house cats, mewed and crawled around their mother. They slipped down the muddy bank of the river and lapped at the water.

"Lucy," Oliver whispered, "do you think that's the same jaguar we saw…"

A solemn silence fell over the river as the baby jaguars drank their fill and scampered back to their mother. One cub slipped on the mud and fell into the river. Its mother, quick to action, dove forward and seized the cub by the scruff of its neck. Despite her powerful jaw being strong enough to break bones, the mother jaguar handled her cub with greatest delicacy as she plopped the young creature back onto dry land.

The cub shook itself dry, and mother led her children back into the bushes, where they disappeared without a trace. "Wow," Lucy said, spellbound.

"Woohoo!" Oliver shouted as he bounced across the runway toward their plane home. "It was a fun trip, but now we'll finally get back to civilization. No more hiking hundreds of miles away from the nearest Wi-Fi connection."

On Lucy's shoulder, Moe wiped his eyes with a wing. "Sniff. Farewell, my beloved Amazon. My motherland, where I roamed when I was a wee chick."

Truthfully, Lucy didn't want to leave, especially after such an epic encounter with a jaguar. Before she boarded the plane, she took a final look at the jungle and inhaled one last breath of the sweet-smelling flowers. *Ah…*

Her tablet went on the fritz. Startled, she answered the call. It was Professor Meridian.

"Salutations, Locators. Hope you're not too comfortable. I've got a new mission for you."

## KEY WORDS FROM PART 1

*aerial imagery, basin, biome, conservationist, corridor, deforestation, endangered species, leaching, meridian, navigate*

## ACROSS

4. *The act or process of cutting down the trees of a forest*

8. *A person who acts for the protection and preservation of the environment and wildlife*

9. *Photographs taken from an aircraft or other flying object that show the earth's surface*

10. *A species of plant or animal that is in danger of becoming extinct*

## DOWN

1. *An area of habitat connecting wildlife populations that are separated by human activities or structures*

2. *Half of an imaginary great circle on the earth's surface that passes through the North and South Poles*

3. *An area that can be classified according to the plants and animals that live in it*

5. *A large area of land drained by a river*

6. *Plan and direct the route of travel, especially by using instruments or maps*

7. *The process of nutrients being removed from soil*

ANDES

PART 2

Instead of home, they flew to the thin, mountainous nation of Chile on the opposite coast of South America. The professor had given them clear instructions: locate an endangered chinchilla herd and protect it from poachers.

"What's a chinchilla?" Oliver asked. "A monstrous lizard? A big, horrible bird?"

"*SQUAWK*," Moe said. "Birds are *not* horrible!"

"Actually…" Lucy perused the articles the professor had sent her about chinchillas. "They're cute, fluffy rodents. They're hunted for their thick coats, and now they're endangered in the wild."

"Rodents? Phew, an easy assignment. A nice change of pace after the last one," Moe said.

"I wouldn't say easy. Chinchillas live two and a half miles above sea level," Lucy said. "Hopefully, you packed your mountaineering gear, because we're going climbing."

"Uh oh," Oliver said.

On her tablet, Lucy brought up the map of South America the professor had sent her. It was supposed to show where to go, but the professor hadn't marked their destination. She had given them some hints, though. It was another test!

Lucy read the professor's hints. The chinchilla herd was located on a mountain 25 miles northeast of the Las Chinchillas National Reserve, in the Coquimbo region of Chile. But where was the Coquimbo region?

# LOCATE COQUIMBO

1. Circle the Coquimbo region.
2. How many regions are there in Chile? ANSWER _____

Arica and Parinacota

Tarapacá

Antofagasta

Atacama

Coquimbo

Valparaíso
Santiago

O'Higgins

Maule
Ñuble

Biobío

Araucanía

Los Ríos

Los Lagos

Aysén

Magallanes

PACIFIC OCEAN

CHILE

BOLIVIA

BRAZIL

PARAGUAY

URUGUAY

ARGENTINA

ATLANTIC OCEAN

Aha, based on the map's labels, she found the Coquimbo region in the upper-middle part of the country. She zoomed the map to show the region in more detail, trying to find Las Chinchillas National Reserve, the only nature reserve in Chile dedicated to chinchillas. According to the professor, the reserve was close to the city of Illapel.

The reserve was pretty small, but Lucy was able to locate it and zoom closer. Next, she had to find the mountain called Cerro Cenicero. It was about 20 miles northeast of the nature reserve, located on the border between the Choapa and Limarí provinces. All these names were starting to confuse her, so she wrote them down to remember.

When she looked at the map, however, she couldn't see Cerro Cenicero labeled *anywhere*. Some maps don't label mountains or other features, because if everything was labeled it would totally clutter the map. She'd have to find the mountain based on other clues and label it herself.

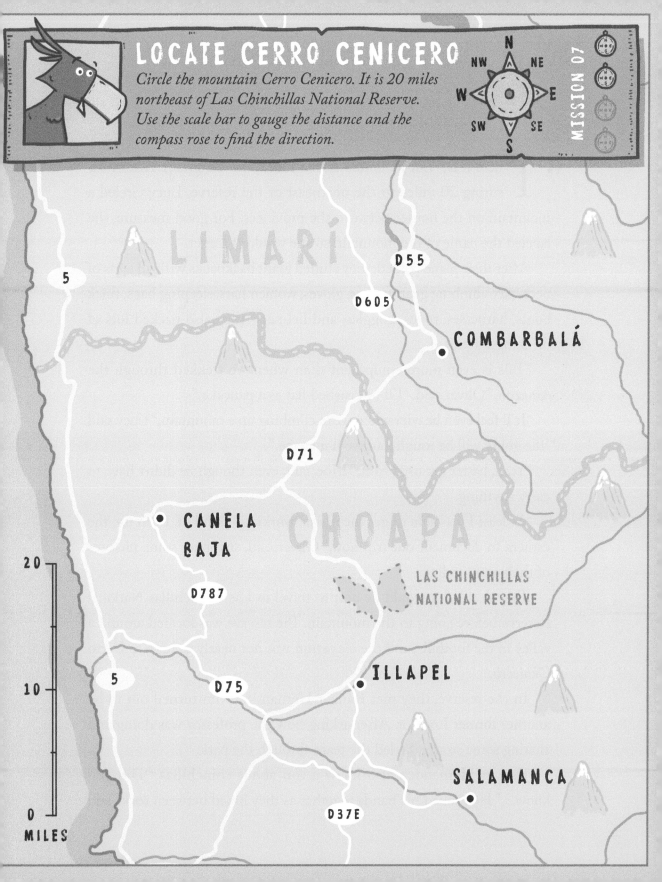

# LOCATE CERRO CENICERO

Circle the mountain Cerro Cenicero. It is 20 miles northeast of Las Chinchillas National Reserve. Use the scale bar to gauge the distance and the compass rose to find the direction.

N
NW    NE
W          E
SW    SE
S

LIMARÍ

5

D55

D605

COMBARBALÁ

D71

CANELA
BAJA

CHOAPA

D787

LAS CHINCHILLAS
NATIONAL RESERVE

20

5

D75

ILLAPEL

10

SALAMANCA

0

MILES

D37E

# CHAPTER 8

"There it is," Lucy shouted as she found the mountain. After measuring 20 miles to the northeast of the reserve, Lucy circled a mountain on the border between the provinces. For good measure, she labeled the name of the mountain so she wouldn't forget.

After their plane landed, they stuffed giant backpacks with all sorts of necessary climbing gear: parkas, gloves, woolen hats, sleeping bags, thick boots, harnesses, ropes, goggles, and helmets. They also packed lots of drinking water.

"This is even more equipment than when we trekked through the Amazon," Oliver said. "I'll be crushed flat as a pancake."

"It'll feel even heavier when we're climbing up a mountain," Lucy said. "The going will be rough, but we'll manage."

"Yeah, better get used to it," Moe said, even though *he* didn't have to carry anything.

"At least I was able to get the phone working—kind of. I can use the camera to document our trip now," Oliver said, snapping some pictures of their surroundings.

They decided it would be best to travel to Las Chinchillas National Reserve before going to the mountain. The reserve was located around a valley in the foothills, and the elevation was not nearly as high as Cerro Cenicero.

In the reserve, they met Ranger Hernandez, who turned out to be another former Locator. After asking how the professor was doing and sharing some stories, he led the team through the park.

Ranger Hernandez also knew a ton about chinchillas. "Did you know…" He rubbed his hands together as they hiked between rocks and

CHINCHILLA

THICKEST FUR OF ALL LAND ANIMALS

LIVES IN HERDS

ENDANGERED: EXTREME RECENT POPULATION LOSS

cacti. "The Andes mountains have lots of volcanoes, so the mountains are often covered in volcanic ash. Chinchillas love to dive in the ash and take dust baths."

"How can you take a bath in *dust?*" Lucy asked. "Don't you just get dirtier?"

Ranger Hernandez gave a hearty laugh. "Ah. The dust is good for the chinchillas' thick, soft fur. It absorbs moisture and keeps them dry, which stops their fur from clumping and matting."

Weird. For chinchillas, a water bath could make them messier than before. Lucy scribbled the ranger's information in her notebook and only looked up when Moe squawked at her to watch out for a cactus she almost walked into.

"Can we see any chinchillas in the reserve?" Lucy asked.

Ranger Hernandez shook his head. "They do live here, but chinchillas are small and like to hide in little crevices and caves, especially during the day. They can be hard to find."

Even though Lucy was disappointed, she reminded herself that their goal was to find chinchillas *outside* the reserve, which were in danger from poachers. But how would they be able to find chinchillas on a remote mountain if they couldn't even find them in a park called Las Chinchillas?

"Chinchillas usually live in the alpine biome, where it's cold and windy, so the chinchillas' thick fur is essential to its survival. Few plants grow there, but there are small roots and grasses that the chinchillas like to eat," explained Ranger Hernandez.

Ranger Hernandez took them to the edge of the reserve and pointed them in the direction of Cerro Cenicero. "Farewell," he said, "and good luck on your journey."

Lucy led the way. The hike got a lot tougher.

"What are we gonna do when we get to this mountain?" Oliver asked. "Climb up and down until we see a chinchilla? That'll take forever. I don't think I can handle it."

"I'm a delicate bird," Moe added. "If I get too cold, my feathers will freeze."

As much as she hated to admit it, they had a point. They'd only get tired if they climbed all over the mountain without a plan. Lucy examined the map of Cerro Cenicero on her tablet, but she couldn't get much information from a top-down view. The mountain was much taller than it was wide, after all.

Lucy brought up a map of the mountain that the professor had sent them before they left. This map showed the mountain, but from the side instead of from above. She needed to identify the most likely place to find chinchillas.

She thought back to the facts Ranger Hernandez had told them. They just needed to determine which elevation level matched the alpine biome on Cerro Cenicero and they could be on their way.

# LOCATE THE ALPINE BIOME

*Circle the alpine biome. Remember what Ranger Hernandez said, and look at the vegetation and terrain to determine the correct elevation.*

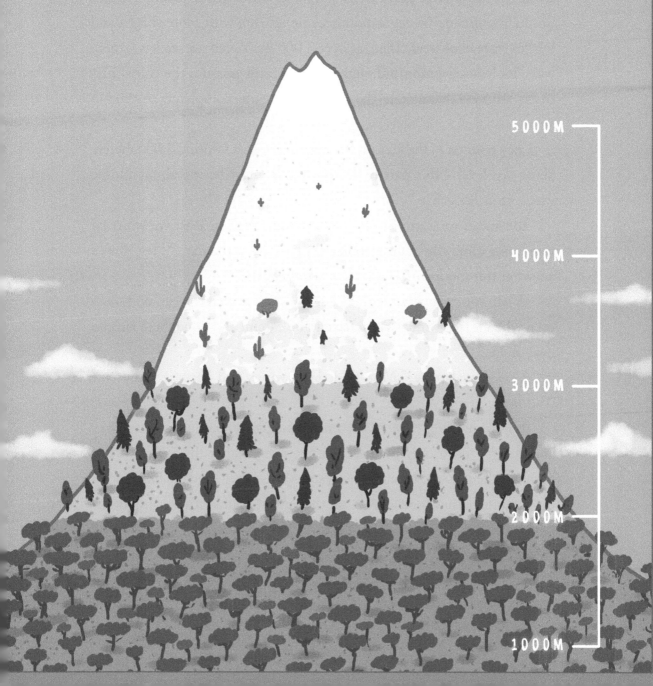

5000M

4000M

3000M

2000M

1000M

As Lucy examined the map, she discovered a pattern. At the base of the mountain, there were trees and other green plants. Farther up the mountain, the vegetation became sparser, with more shrubs and bushes instead of trees. Then, at over 3,000 meters above sea level, there was a lot less vegetation, although there was still grass for the chinchillas to eat. Above 5,000 meters, the mountain became completely covered in snow.

Lucy pointed to the area on the map between 3,000 and 5,000 meters above sea level. "This part of the mountain must be the alpine biome where chinchillas live."

"You mean we gotta go close to the top? Well, at least we won't be wandering aimlessly." Oliver took another look at the map. "Hey, there's snow on this mountain. But it's not winter, is it?"

"When you get up that high," Lucy said, "it's so cold you can find snow even when it isn't winter. We'll have to be careful and hope there isn't an avalanche."

"A—a—avalanche?" Moe folded his wings and became indignant. "This is *not* in my contract."

They began their hike up the mountain. The steep slopes were rocky and craggy, and it only got more difficult the higher they went. Wind buffeted them as they trudged onward. When they made it halfway up the mountain, they took a break on the flattest boulder they could find.

Oliver flopped down with a heavy sigh. "We haven't seen a single chinchilla yet."

"We're not high enough yet." Lucy consulted the map of the mountain. Based on the shrubs poking out between occasional clumps of snow, she suspected they needed to climb for a few more hours. Amazing that a mountain could contain so many different plants, species, and ecosystems in such a small area.

Suddenly, Oliver pointed. "Hey, Lucy, look over there."

Not far from them stood a fluffy, long-necked animal that looked kind of like a camel, but without a hump. It was a llama! Lucy flipped through her notebook while Oliver and Moe inched closer. The llama didn't just *look* like a camel. It was closely related, even though the two species lived on opposite sides of the world. Ancient civilizations in the Andes domesticated the llama in order to carry things up the steep cliffs. This llama seemed like it didn't belong to anyone, though. It proudly stepped among the rocks with its thin, hoofed feet and nibbled some shrubs.

"Hmm, this isn't right," Lucy said. "According to my notes, wild llamas live in herds. Why's this one alone?"

Moe took flight. "*SQUAWK…* Why don't we ask it?" Before Lucy could stop him, he cupped his wings around his beak and shouted, "Hey, scruffy, what're you doing all by yourself?"

The llama startled at the sudden shout. It leaped off the large rock it had been standing on and landed on a nearby ledge. The rock it had jumped off of began to wobble and shake. Then, it tumbled down the ridge.

*Bang, crack, smash!* The large rock bounced several times as it fell. Lucy, Oliver, Moe, and even the llama watched it drop, until it became only a tiny speck far, far below. Finally, the speck settled at the base of a deep canyon.

For a moment, everything was silent. Then, the mountainside rumbled.

Dirt, dust, and snow slid down the ridge. At first, only small rocks joined the slide, but soon a chain reaction started and larger stones rushed past. Lucy realized what was happening, and it was *bad*.

"Landslide!" she shouted. "We have to get somewhere safe before the whole mountainside crashes down."

Nearby, she saw a narrow cave in the side of the mountain. The cave seemed sturdy—although she had no way to know for sure. It was the best place she could find, and she didn't have time to worry about it.

She seized Oliver's arm. "This way!" They ran toward the cave as larger rocks fell. Moe squawked in fright and flew after them as they reached the cave and took cover. It was a small cave, but they fit inside with room to spare.

Then they realized they had forgotten someone—the llama. It bolted side to side, baaing in dismay as rocks dropped around it.

"Over here," Oliver shouted. "Come in here, it's safe."

The llama perked its head up at the sound of his voice. It bounded toward the cave, deftly dodging debris. It skittered inside, taking up the small space they had left. Lucy and Oliver were squished against its soft and fluffy body.

Sand, rocks, and even boulders continued to tumble down the slopes for what felt like eternity. Then, more suddenly than Lucy expected, the shaking stopped. Finally, everything became quiet.

The cave entrance was half-blocked by rubble, but not enough to stop Lucy and Oliver from crawling outside. "Careful," Oliver called out. "It might not be stable yet."

Lucy examined the landscape. It had totally changed. She shouldn't have been surprised—a huge segment of the mountain had basically moved from one spot to another.

Moe let out a loud squawk. "Freedom! It's no good to keep a bird cooped up. And that stinky llama, PEW."

"That's what you're complaining about?" Oliver said. "The smell? Moe, we almost got buried alive."

"Correction: *You* almost got buried alive. I could have flown away at any time. I only stayed because you kids need avian supervision."

Oliver and Lucy rolled their eyes. The llama stuck its head out of the cave and snorted in Moe's face, which caused the bird to squawk in dismay.

Although the rockslide had ended, Lucy was worried. She brought out her tablet and looked over the map. The landscape had completely changed, and her map didn't look *anything* like the real terrain anymore. It wasn't safe to climb on the debris from the landslide. They needed to find a new route to the top of the mountain.

# DESTINATION: SUMMIT

*Draw a path up the mountain that navigates the team from the base to the mountain's summit.*

SUMMIT

BASE

# FIND A NEW PATH

*Wow, that was a close one! An avalanche has changed the terrain. Draw a new path for the team from the base to the mountain's summit.*

SUMMIT

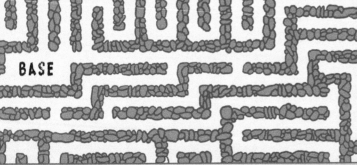

BASE

"There we go," Lucy said, as she finally finished editing her map with the changes caused by the landslide. The new route was clear, but less direct than the old route. She showed Oliver the path and expected a groan, but he seemed surprisingly eager.

"I just got an idea." Oliver turned to the llama and whistled. "Hey, c'mere, girl," he said, as though he were talking to a pet dog. The llama stared at him, then blinked and crawled out of the cave. She carefully approached Oliver, who stroked her fluffy white coat. "Hey there, girl… nothing to be afraid of…"

"What are you doing?" Lucy asked.

"I wanna see if this nice llama wants to carry my equipment."

"That won't work," Lucy said. "You can't get a wild llama to carry your stuff for you."

Oliver kept stroking. The llama didn't seem too afraid of him. "This one likes us, though. We helped her during the landslide."

Despite Lucy's expectations, Oliver managed to convince the llama to carry his backpack. They continued up the mountain, Lucy leading the way and the llama right behind her. She had to admit that she *was* a rather friendly llama. Even Moe started to get along with her.

Although the new route was longer, it took only a few more hours to reach the alpine biome near the top of Cerro Cenicero. It looked exactly as expected: a rocky, windy slope with only tiny patches of grass growing here and there. It didn't seem like anything could live there, let alone an entire herd of rodents.

"All right, keep your eyes open for chinchillas," Lucy said. "We need to find the herd and then contact the professor."

"This is where I come in," Moe said. "From the air, it'll be much easier to spot anything moving around."

The parrot flapped his wings and took flight. He soared over the mountain, his bright green plumage contrasting against the drab gray landscape. Soon, he disappeared from view.

After several minutes, he returned. "Found 'em. A whole horde of the little beasts, just past those rocks over there."

Lucy took off as soon as he pointed. She couldn't wait to see real chinchillas in the wild. But as she got closer, she slowed down and approached more carefully. She didn't want to startle the chinchillas, and it would be best if they didn't hear her coming. She motioned to Oliver and the llama for quiet and peeked her head over the rocks.

At first, she didn't see anything. Only more of the same dirt and snow. But then, a fluffy little thing darted into a crevice—a chinchilla. Lucy started to see more of them, gathered in groups and nibbling on grass. Three, five, eight, twelve…tons of them.

She took out her tablet and called Professor Meridian. When she answered with a loud, "My indomitable students!" Lucy had to tell her to quiet down.

"We found the chinchillas, Professor. A whole herd of them. At least 30, and probably more hiding nearby." She pointed the tablet toward the chinchillas so she could see.

The professor clapped her hands. "Aha, how exciting. There's more than I expected. I'm recording your footage now. We'll be able to use this video evidence to prove that there's a substantial population on this mountain. We can take steps to have the area protected so no poachers can come around."

Lucy pumped her fist in the air. Yes! It seemed like they might be

# LOCATE CHINCHILLA HABITAT

*Connect the dots with the same values to create contours. Do not cross the lines. You will have three continuous lines (the 2000s, 3000s, and 4000s).*

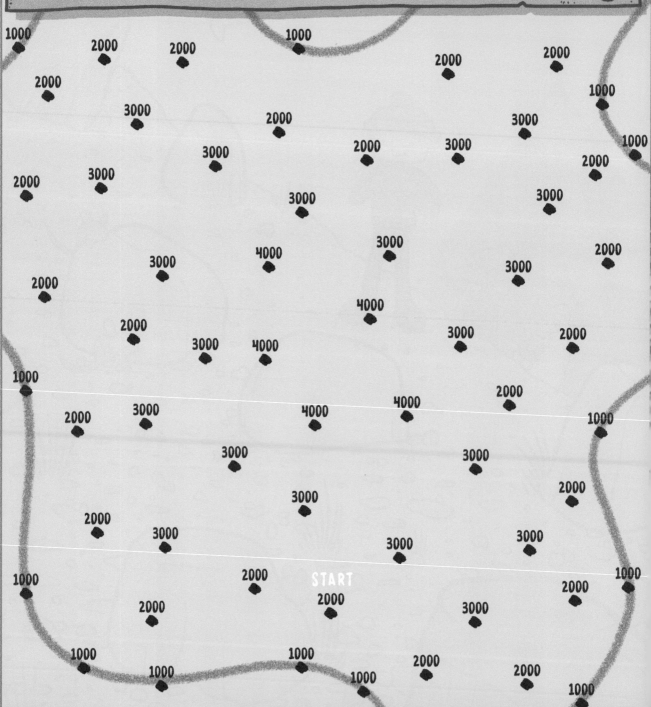

able to make a difference and help defend the endangered chinchilla population.

"I have one final request, Locators. It'll be best if we can give the authorities a map showing the chinchillas' habitat range. That way, it'll be easier to determine the area to protect."

"But the chinchillas don't live in only this exact spot," Oliver said. "They probably move around over the mountain. It'll take weeks to track them and find everywhere they live. We don't have enough supplies."

"What if I told you there was another way? I'm sending you a new kind of map. It might be a little different from the maps you're used to, but don't worry—everything will be explained."

The map showed up on the screen. The professor was right—it looked *really* weird.

"That map shows Cerro Cenicero," said Professor Meridian. "But not in a usual way. The number next to each dot represents the elevation at that exact spot. This is what's known as a **topographic** map."

Lucy was beginning to understand. The dots with higher numbers were higher—they represented the top of the mountain. Meanwhile, the lower numbers represented the mountain's base. "But how does this help us, Professor?"

"You already know chinchillas prefer to live in the alpine biome," the professor explained. "And you also know that the alpine biome starts at 3,000 meters—or about 2 miles—above sea level. If you use that map to find all the areas within the alpine biome, you can predict the chinchilla habitat without having to follow them for days."

"I think I get it," Lucy said. "All right, let's find out where the chinchillas live."

# CHAPTER 11

"There," Lucy exclaimed, once she and Oliver had predicted the area where chinchillas lived on the mountain. She sent the map back to the professor.

"Yes, very good," Professor Meridian said. "Of course, this is only an estimate of the chinchilla range. But when I send this to the Chilean authorities, they can use it as a starting point to protect this area."

Lucy surveyed the mountain. The chinchillas continued to hop, dash, and frolic among the rocky crevices. Some burrowed into the dust and rolled around, taking what Ranger Hernandez had called a "dust bath."

It shocked Lucy that anyone would want to hurt such adorable creatures, but she knew from her notes that the chinchillas' soft, fluffy fur was in high demand for coats and clothing. If the government protected this remote area, as they had Las Chinchillas National Reserve, then this herd of cute critters could continue to live in peace.

The next day, it was time to go back down the mountain. They said goodbye to the chinchillas and set off for the foothills. Oliver's llama—whom he'd named Olivia—continued to carry his bag on the way down.

When they reached the halfway point of the mountain, not far from where they first met the llama, Olivia suddenly stopped. She looked around the rocky area, and then started to trot in a different direction. Oliver and Lucy chased after her—and Oliver's stuff—but they only managed to catch up when the llama stopped at the top of a small canyon. In the valley that stretched beyond, a herd of llamas grazed.

"That must be her family," Lucy said. The llama herd reminded her of the chinchilla herd, especially because both animals had such big, fluffy coats.

"Does…does this mean it's goodbye?" Oliver sniffled and wiped away a tear as he turned to Olivia. Olivia snorted and nuzzled Oliver's out-stretched hand.

Moe landed on Lucy's shoulder and started to bawl. "I can't take these tragic endings."

Oliver gave Olivia one final hug, took one last selfie together, and then saw the llama off as it bounded down the canyon to its friends and family.

Lucy placed a hand on Oliver's shoulder. "It's all right, buddy," she said. "It's all right."

Though it was sad to see Olivia go, Lucy knew she belonged with her family in the wild. Being a Locator wasn't easy, but it *was* worthwhile, especially after an adventure like this. There was nothing like helping to save such wonderful critters. They'd made a difference in the world!

Lucy took one last glance at the amazing view, and then climbed down the rest of the mountain to await their next mission from Professor Meridian.

| | | | | | | | | | | | | | | |
|---|---|---|---|---|---|---|---|---|---|---|---|---|---|---|
| O | R | E | S | E | R | V | E | P | P | K | N | U | S | D | D | Y |
| D | P | E | A | I | L | H | U | D | R | A | S | R | O | O | G | S |
| S | C | K | V | X | J | U | Q | U | U | O | I | E | Z | R | J | U |
| A | G | M | A | E | G | L | I | E | E | K | V | H | T | P | P | R |
| J | O | E | L | E | V | A | T | I | O | N | T | I | G | O | C | V |
| J | K | D | A | N | L | L | E | Y | H | F | L | W | N | A | Z | E |
| M | O | U | N | T | A | I | N | E | E | R | I | N | G | C | E | Y |
| N | E | A | C | E | P | O | I | O | N | O | A | V | N | H | E | C |
| F | N | D | H | H | S | W | L | O | I | I | U | X | N | E | W | R |
| A | F | A | E | E | C | G | L | E | V | F | F | T | S | R | H | C |
| W | I | T | O | P | O | G | R | A | P | H | I | C | K | I | K | R |

|  |  |
|---|---|
| AVALANCHE | The sudden rush of a large amount of snow, ice, or rocks down a mountain |
| AVIAN | Of or relating to birds |
| ELEVATION | The height to which something rises or is raised, or its height above sea level or ground level |
| MOUNTAINEERING | The sport of climbing to high points in mountainous regions |
| POACHER | One who illegally hunts on another's property |
| PROVINCE | A division of a country |
| RESERVE | The area of land that is protected and managed in order to preserve the habitat and flora |
| SURVEY | To examine carefully |
| TOPOGRAPHIC | A type of map that uses contour lines to show the shape of the earth's surface |

# PART 3

Rio de Janeiro

# CHAPTER 12

"Rio de Janeiro," Oliver shouted as he bounded off the plane. After hours of flying, they'd finally arrived. The sunny city stretched along the coast, nestled between the Atlantic Ocean and the mountains. The densely packed skyscrapers reminded Lucy of the Amazon rain forest, which had also seemed to go on forever. But instead of animals, people lived here.

"Come on, Moe, let's find a Wi-Fi hot spot," Oliver said. For once, he was eager to go somewhere. "I haven't been on the internet for weeks."

"Boring! I'm hitting the beach instead. I have to work on my tan," Moe said.

They had only taken a few steps off the runway when Lucy's tablet rang. It was Professor Meridian.

"Hello there, my eager adventurers. I bet you're all wondering why I've sent you to this beautiful seaside city, aren't you?"

"To go to the beach, right?" Oliver said. He looked at his friends for confirmation, but when nobody said anything, he whispered, "We're not going to the beach, are we…"

"I've got a much better idea," the professor said. "Today, I want you to travel to one of the few remnants of the Atlantic coastal forest in Brazil."

The professor struck a pose, as though waiting for her students to erupt in celebration. But Lucy, Oliver, and Moe only exchanged confused glances. The Atlantic coastal forest? Lucy had never heard of that.

"Professor, what do you mean?" Lucy asked. "What's the Atlantic coastal forest, and how is it different from the rain forest?"

"The Atlantic coastal forest is a unique **ecoregion** that covers the coast of Brazil. It doesn't get quite as much rain as the Amazon, and the climate's a bit cooler. As such, the Atlantic forest has very different plants and animals, including many that don't live anywhere else."

"So if the Atlantic forest is destroyed, those animals won't have anywhere else to live," Lucy said. "That means it's especially important to protect."

But it wasn't that simple. As the professor explained, a massive amount of Brazil's human population lived in nearby Rio de Janeiro. A lot of forest had been cut down to make room for cities and farms, and the little that remained was in major danger.

"Your mission is simple, intrepid Locators. I need you to journey to one of the remaining pieces of the Atlantic forest and determine how it can be protected."

# IDENTIFY MAP FEATURES

*Write the four main types of things (map features) that you see on the map.*

1.                          2.

3.                          4.

VASSOURAS

117

495

127

MIGUEL PEREIRA

115

PETRÓPOLIS

MENDES

125

107

040

JAPERI

493

MAGÉ

QUEIMADOS

493

SEROPÉDICA

116

DUQUE DE CAXIAS

101

493

NOVA IGUAÇUO

105

ITAGUAÍ

SÃO GONÇALO

101

RIO DE JANEIRO

It didn't sound as simple as the professor said, but Lucy was game for the challenge. She hoisted her backpack onto her shoulders and prepared to set out. "Just give us a map, Professor."

Lucy received a new map on her tablet. Oliver and Moe gathered around to look. The first thing they needed to do was find their current location: Rio de Janeiro.

It didn't take long to find the city. But when Lucy zoomed in closer, she was surprised she didn't see the forest anywhere.

Oliver seemed to have trouble, too. "Didn't she say the forest was close to Rio? But it's not there."

"The professor must have made a mistake," Lucy said. "We learned in class that there are many different types of maps, and they sometimes show totally different things, even when they're focused on the same place."

"Like that elevation map the professor gave us for the mountain with the chinchillas?" Oliver said.

"Exactly," Lucy said. "Let's figure out what this map shows, so we can tell the professor. Then she can give us a map that shows the forest instead."

# CHAPTER 13

Once they'd figured out the problem, they called Professor Meridian and explained that the map she'd sent them showed cities and roads, but not the Atlantic coastal forest.

"*SQUAWK*," Moe said. "In short, this map shows where people live, not where *animals* live."

"You're so sharp, students," said the professor. "Indeed, instead of a physical map, I sent you a political map."

A political map? Lucy remembered hearing that term in class. She checked her notes. "Aha! A political map shows features that were created by people: countries, states, cities, roads, and so on. Meanwhile, a physical map shows natural features: mountains, valleys, rivers, and forests. Some maps show both kinds of features, but most maps are one or the other."

In the time it took Lucy to read through her notes, Moe had gone to a nearby street vendor. He returned with a bag of popcorn and munched handfuls while Lucy, Oliver, and the professor figured out what to do next.

"Unfortunately, I don't have a physical map of Rio de Janeiro right now," Professor Meridian said. "I might be able to find one, but it'll take time. After all, you'd usually use a political map to show a city."

Lucy didn't want to wait. The professor said the Atlantic forests were in severe danger, which meant the sooner they got to work, the better. "Are you sure there's no other way for us to find the forest?"

The entire time, Oliver had been thinking deeply. "Hmm… What if we knew its absolute location?"

"Its what?" Lucy said.

Oliver seemed to realize he had put himself in the spotlight and bit his lip, a little embarrassed. "I mean, so far, we figured out where we need to go based on its location **relative** to something else. Let's say we needed to go to a mountain, and we knew that mountain was 15 miles north of Rio de Janeiro. That would be the mountain's relative location."

Lucy thought about what Oliver said. When you had a relative location, you needed to know the location of something else to find the location of the thing you wanted. In Oliver's example, they would need to know the location of Rio de Janeiro first, and then they could find the mountain.

"Absolute location is different," Oliver continued. "**Cartographers** hundreds of years ago gave every location in the world a unique pair of numbers to tell them apart. These numbers are called **coordinates**."

Numbers! No wonder Oliver knew about this—math was one of his best subjects.

"Numbers for every place in the world?" Moe said. "I'd sure hate to be the person who had that job. It'd take forever."

"They didn't go around the world giving each place a number one by one, Moe," Oliver said. "They used math to figure it out."

"Oliver, you're *absolute*-ly right. I am so proud of you right now." Professor Meridian pointed to the old-fashioned globe on her desk. The globe had several lines running across it. Some lines went up and down, while others went left and right. "Each of these lines has a number. To find the absolute location of any place in the world, just find the two lines that touch it. The numbers of each line will be that place's coordinates."

The part of the globe that she pointed to showed New York City, the biggest city in the United States. Lucy looked at the lines that intersected the city: the horizontal (left and right) line said 40° N, and the vertical (up and down) line said 75° W. "So the coordinates for New York City are 40° N and 75° W?"

"Exactly," the professor said. "The *N* stands for north, and the *W* stands for west. That means that New York City is in both the northern half of the world and the western half."

"Geez, this math stuff is real complicated," Moe said. "What's it got to do with anything?"

"This is how we'll find the Atlantic coastal forest," Oliver explained. "Professor, can you give us the forest's coordinates?"

The professor flipped through one of her books and read: "The forest is located at about 22° 35′ S, 43° 15′ W."

Lucy scribbled the coordinates down in her notes. Now she just needed to check the map and find the forest.

# USE THE GRID

*Find where the Atlanic coastal forest is located by marking an X at the intersection of 22° 35' S and 43° 15' W. Use the numbers (coordinates) along the side and bottom of the map.*

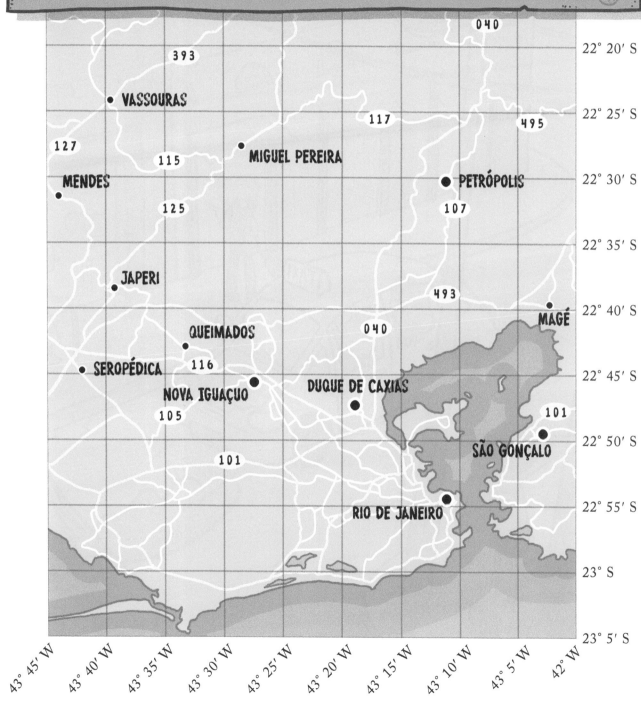

040

393

VASSOURAS

22° 20' S

117

495

22° 25' S

127

115

MIGUEL PEREIRA

MENDES

PETRÓPOLIS

22° 30' S

125

107

22° 35' S

JAPERI

493

MAGÉ

22° 40' S

QUEIMADOS

040

SEROPÉDICA

116

22° 45' S

NOVA IGUAÇUO

DUQUE DE CAXIAS

101

105

SÃO GONÇALO

22° 50' S

101

RIO DE JANEIRO

22° 55' S

23° S

23° 5' S

43° 45' W  43° 40' W  43° 35' W  43° 30' W  43° 25' W  43° 20' W  43° 15' W  43° 10' W  43° 5' W  42° W

"I've got it," Lucy said, hastily tossing her notebook and tablet into her bag. "The forest is north of Rio de Janeiro and west of Petrópolis. According to the scale bar, it's about 20 miles from where we are now, so we'd better get hiking."

She grabbed Oliver's arm and dragged him along. "Wait, Lucy, come on. We're not in the Amazon rain forest or the Andes Mountains. We can take a taxicab."

"Oh, right," Lucy said. "A taxi, it is."

It didn't take long to find one in the bustling Rio de Janeiro streets. They cut north across the city and passed through what felt like hundreds of neighborhoods, Oliver filming most of the way on his phone. "This is incredible."

Finally, they reached the Atlantic forest north of Rio de Janeiro—and Lucy was shocked to see that the forest started exactly where the city ended. One moment, they drove down a street, surrounded by houses on all sides. The next moment, the houses were replaced by sprawling hills covered in trees. It was almost as if the forest was part of Rio de Janeiro.

They paid the taxi driver and stepped out onto the border between the forest and the city. Lucy noticed that the forest was located mostly on hills, while the buildings were located in the valleys between them. That made sense, since people don't usually live on mountains. It was also a good thing, because it meant that what remained of the forest was relatively safe. At least, that was what she thought—until she noticed that houses were starting to be built on some of the foothills.

"Oh no," she said. "The professor was right. This forest really is in danger."

# GOLDEN LION TAMARIN

SLEEPS IN DIFFERENT DENS EACH DAY

LIVES IN GROUPS OF 2 TO 8 MEMBERS

ENDANGERED: SEVERE HABITAT LOSS

"Are those people really going to live on the side of the mountain?" Oliver asked. "Man, it was hard enough climbing a mountain once. I couldn't imagine living on one."

Moe flew to a nearby tree and perched on one of the higher branches. He still had his bag of popcorn from the Rio de Janeiro street vendor. "You humans sure have problems with altitude. Now if birds ruled the world—"

Something bright orange darted out of the bushes and snatched Moe's popcorn bag. Moe squawked and flapped his wings at the thief. The orange critter darted away and jumped to the next tree. It held the popcorn bag in its hands while it dangled upside down from a branch.

"A monkey!" Lucy took out her notes and flipped through them. "Specifically, a golden lion tamarin."

"A lion? That thing?" Oliver said.

"They call it a golden lion tamarin because of its mane of golden-orange fur," Lucy said. "It's not related to actual lions, of course."

"I call it a thief," Moe said. "Gimme back my lunch!" He swooped at the tamarin, but it quickly dropped to another branch and scampered back and forth, munching fistfuls of popcorn.

"According to my notes, it's only found here in the Atlantic coastal forest," Lucy said. "Due to deforestation, it's an endangered species."

"Oh, you bet it's in danger." Moe dove with his talons bared for the bag of popcorn. Moments before he reached it, the tamarin pulled it away, causing Moe to fly straight into a tree trunk.

*Thwack!*

The tamarin stuck out its tongue and scampered deeper into the forest. Moe shook his feathers and flew after the mischievous monkey.

"Wait, Moe," Lucy said. "If you go in by yourself, you'll get lost." But Moe had already disappeared. Lucy and Oliver raced after him.

The forest was covered in brush and ferns. It was not quite as over-grown as the Amazon. She chased after the sound of the monkey's squeaks and Moe's squawks.

Soon, she was totally exhausted. She leaned against a tree and caught her breath. It was crazy that such a huge forest could be so close to a big city.

Oliver flopped onto the ground nearby. "Nobody…said anything…about chasing monkeys…*hurk*…"

When Lucy looked up, something orange and furry was hanging right in front of her face—the tamarin. Its feet clutched a branch and in its hands was Moe's popcorn bag.

"Hey there, fella," Lucy said. "You're giving our friend a lot of trouble, aren't you?"

The tamarin dropped the bag of popcorn, climbed back into the trees, and dashed away. The next moment, Moe burst out of the bushes.

"*SQUAWK!* Where'd the little rascal go?" He noticed his bag on the ground and flapped toward it. "Ah, I see it was smart enough to give back what it stole. At least it hasn't lost all respect for authority." He picked up the popcorn bag and immediately squawked. "It's empty!"

Their antics were interrupted by Lucy's tablet, which started to ring. It was the professor. "Salutations, Locators. Have you reached the forest yet?"

"We didn't just reach it, we're *inside* it," Lucy said.

"I see. Well, a little monkeying around never hurt anyone. But now, it's time to get back to your original task. I managed to find a map that shows both the Atlantic coastal forest and the city around it."

"A little late," Moe said.

"Yes, but you can use this map along with your observations on the ground to solve some tough problems." The professor brought the map up on the screen. It was a mix of a physical and a political map. "I need you to think critically about this map and describe the patterns you see."

"Patterns?" Lucy asked. "What kind of patterns?"

"Patterns of the city's development. Surely, you've seen the buildings near the forest, yes?"

Lucy remembered the hillside that was cleared for new houses. "So you want us to find the places where there's construction?"

"Not just that—I want you to think about places where there might be construction soon. Even if the forest itself isn't cut down, having so many homes close to the forest can hurt the fragile ecosystem with pollution and trash. To better protect the forest, we need to understand the areas that need the *most* protection."

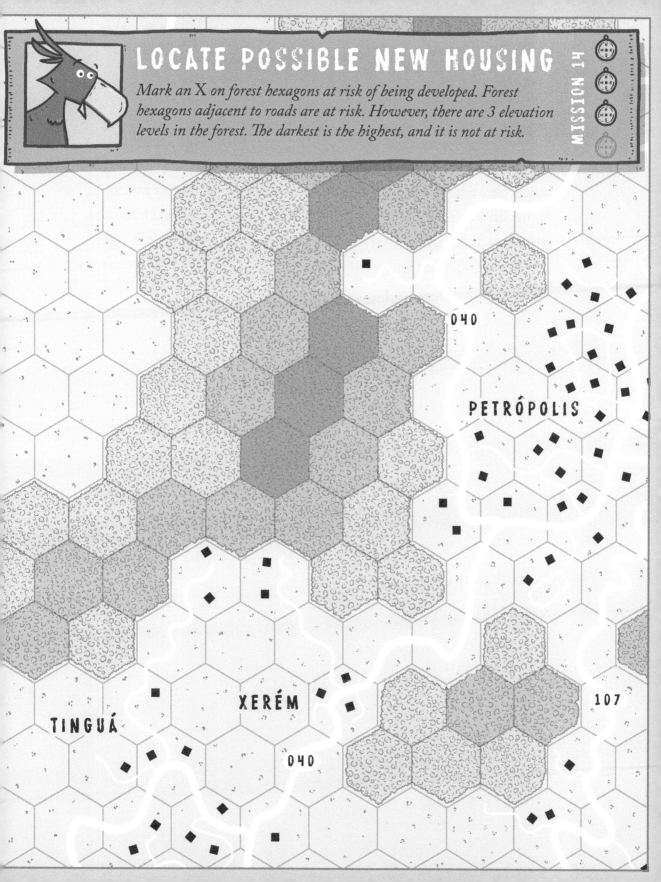

# LOCATE POSSIBLE NEW HOUSING

*Mark an X on forest hexagons at risk of being developed. Forest hexagons adjacent to roads are at risk. However, there are 3 elevation levels in the forest. The darkest is the highest, and it is not at risk.*

040

PETRÓPOLIS

XERÉM

107

TINGUÁ

040

It made sense to Lucy. If they could find patterns where houses were being built, then they could predict future construction. This must be what the professor meant by thinking critically.

Lucy looked closer at the map. Usually, houses were built in the flat valleys between the hills, but when there was no room left, they were built on the hillsides, too. Also, houses were usually built near other buildings and roads. If she considered that, she should have a good idea of where new houses would be built.

# CHAPTER 15

After studying the map, Lucy thought she had found some places where new houses might be built. "The highest-risk area is Petrópolis, where there's already a ton of buildings near the forest," she explained to the team. "The area around the highway BR-040 is a place where houses might be built, too."

"I think I get it," Oliver said. "There are also the small towns just south of the forest, like Tinguá and Xerém. It'd make sense if they built more houses there, because there's empty space around them."

"Overall, the southern and eastern sides of the forest are probably most at risk," Lucy said. "Especially the eastern side. There aren't as many people north of the forest, and the ones who do live there are pretty far from the forest's edge."

"Shrewd observations," the professor said. "Of course, when you have to think critically, answers might not be as clear-cut as a simple right or wrong. Now, one more question—"

Moe leaped up and squawked loudly. "It's back. IT'S BACK!"

An orange blur sped across the tree branch overhead. The golden lion tamarin. It swooped down from the branch and wrapped its little hands around the tablet. Lucy was so surprised she didn't have time to react before it pulled the tablet away and swung back into the trees.

"It has the professor," Oliver cried out.

"Oh my," the professor said. "It seems I've been kidnapped." She waved her arms for help as the monkey made off with the tablet.

Even if it wasn't really the professor being taken,
they needed the tablet to finish their mission. The tamarin
danced up and down on its branch, gloating over them. "Give that back!"
Lucy shouted.

"I guess the little thief's ready for round two," Moe said.

"Wait, you guys," Oliver said. "If we chase it, there's no way we can
catch it. It's got the home field advantage."

Lucy, who had been ready to climb up a tree herself, realized Oliver
was right. "But what do we do?"

"Tamarins are pretty smart, aren't they?" Oliver rummaged through
his backpack. "How about we try a trade?" He pulled out a small, metal
object. It was a compass.

Oliver held the compass toward the tamarin. The tamarin focused its
attention on the shiny object and took a few steps closer along its tree
branch. It seemed interested in the compass, but it still clutched the tablet.

"Come on over, buddy," Oliver said. "If you hand me that tablet, you
can have this cool gizmo. What do you think? Nice, huh?" He shook the
compass, causing the dial to wobble.

The tamarin seemed excited now. It hopped down from its tree, ran up to Oliver, and held out one hand as if to ask for the compass.

"Nope, it's a trade," Oliver said. It had seemed like a crazy idea at first, but it was working. "You gotta hand over the tablet if you want this compass."

At once, the tamarin drew back its hand and clutched the tablet tightly. It looked as if it would run away, but then it reconsidered. It placed the tablet on the ground and held both hands out.

Oliver handed the compass over and the tamarin scurried back up the tree. Lucy snatched the tablet as quickly as possible. "Great work, Oliver."

"You saved me," Professor Meridian said. "Who knows where that critter might have taken me if not for your quick thinking, Oliver."

"Don't mention it." Oliver rubbed the back of his head and grinned. He seemed a little embarrassed to receive such praise. "So, you said you had one more task for us, Professor?"

"That's right, team. Last time, you predicted where new homes will be built near the forest. Knowing where there might be deforestation is important, but that's only part of the equation. If we want to increase the size of the Atlantic Forest, there's only one thing we can do."

Lucy snapped her fingers. "Plant more trees."

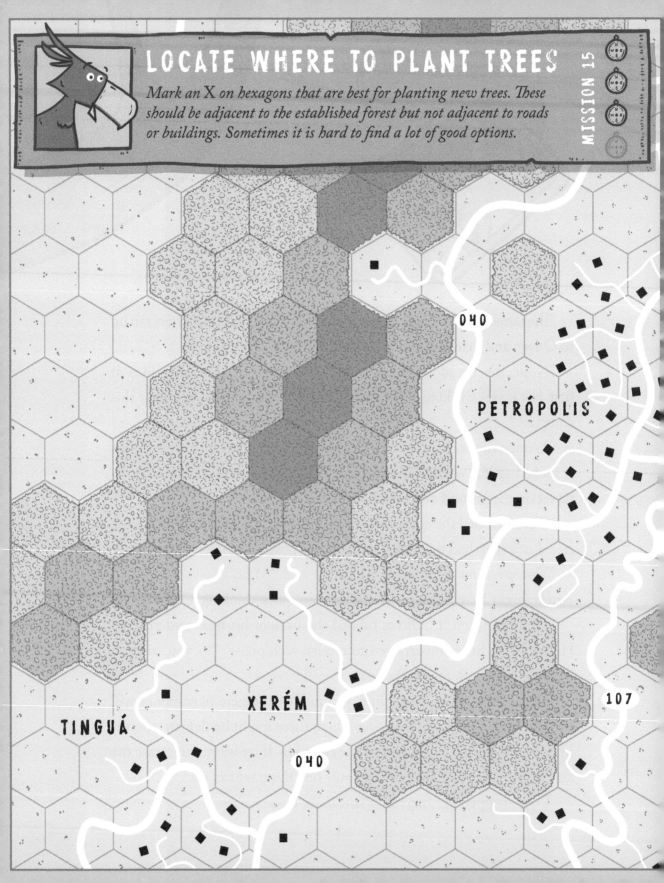

# LOCATE WHERE TO PLANT TREES

*Mark an X on hexagons that are best for planting new trees. These should be adjacent to the established forest but not adjacent to roads or buildings. Sometimes it is hard to find a lot of good options.*

040

PETRÓPOLIS

107

XERÉM

TINGUÁ

040

"Exactly. Habitat restoration is as important as habitat protection when it comes to endangered areas such as the Atlantic coastal forest. The soil loses fewer nutrients than in the rain forest, so it's possible to regrow the trees. But, as always, the big question is: Where?"

Where was right! With Rio de Janeiro and other nearby cities getting bigger, there were fewer and fewer places to plant trees. Professor Meridian sent them another map. It was similar to the previous map, but it marked the places where cities were growing. Somewhere, there had to be places to plant new trees. Right?

# CHAPTER 16

Lucy thought hard about the professor's question. Where *should* they plant new trees? "Well, the city seems to be growing from the south of the forest. But north of the forest there seem to be fewer people."

"The area north of the forest also has a bunch of hills," Oliver added. "That means it's less likely that people will live there in the future."

"*SQUAWK!* There are hills south of the forest, too. Why not plant trees on them, and let the humans live in the valleys?"

It seemed like a good idea… But then Lucy realized something. "If you only plant trees on the hills, then you'll create a lot of small, fragmented forests. If the forest is fragmented, then animals will have to travel through places with people to get around, and that's dangerous. Remember the jaguars? You can already see a situation like that east of the forest, in Petrópolis."

"There's also some open land west of the forest," Oliver said, pointing at the map. "Why not there?"

"You're right, there's empty land there," Lucy said. "But there's also a big highway. New houses might be built there soon, and even if they aren't, animals will have to cross a dangerous road. Still, that's probably a better place than south or east of the forest."

"Oh-ho, excellent answers, students," the professor said from the tablet. "I can tell you're really thinking with maps now. Based on your analysis, the best places to plant new trees are north and west of the Atlantic forest. Of course, even then, it's easier said than done."

"What do you mean, Professor?" Lucy asked, even though she knew she wouldn't like the answer.

"Although those areas might seem empty on the map, they could actually be farms or ranches owned by other people. It's not as simple as just going there and planting some seeds."

Lucy groaned. After all that work, it seemed like there were even *more* maps to analyze if they wanted to make a difference. But if it was easy, then someone probably would have done it already.

"I guess I know how we're spending the rest of our time in Rio de Janeiro," Lucy said.

"Going to the beach?" Oliver said in a hopeful voice.

"No way. We'll scout out the locations we found on the map and see if it's really possible to plant new Atlantic forest there."

Oliver fell to his knees, lifted his arms to the sky, and let out the longest, loudest groan Lucy had ever heard. "And we were so close," he said. "We were *so* close to the beach."

Moe landed on a tree branch and puffed out his chest. "At least now I'll get a rematch with that silly monkey. I'll show it what's what. You don't wanna see me when I'm angry, I'll—Hey, wait, what?"

As he boasted, the bushes around him started to rustle and shake. Suddenly, not one but *six* golden lion tamarins burst out of the leaves and surrounded Moe on all sides. Moe squawked in terror as the little orange monkeys grabbed him and hoisted him overhead. The monkeys danced and squeaked as they ran off into the trees, carrying Moe with them.

"Hey, you! Put me down this in-stant! I'll teach you a thing or two! I'll fight the lot of ya! Just put me down, will you? Help, heeeeeeelp!!"

Lucy and Oliver exchanged a look and then set off to rescue their silly parrot.

*Remember to check Part 3 for the key words if you need help!*

# RAHOGPATRCER

*A person who draws or makes maps*

# IOBVTANOSER

*An act of watching someone or something carefully in order to gain information*

# TORDOANCISE

*A pair of numbers that identify a point on a map*

# CHYLASIP PAM

*A map that shows physical features such as mountains, rivers, and lakes*

# TOSEBULA

*Referring to the location of a place based on a fixed point on earth*

# IIAOLLTPC AMP

*A map that shows government boundaries for countries, states, and towns*

# VLIEAETR

*Referring to the position of a place or entity based on its location with respect to other locations*

# NEEROIOCG

*An area of land or water containing geographically distinct species, natural communities, and environmental conditions*

# PART 4

# CHAPTER 17

After a few more days in Rio de Janeiro, where they'd found several real possibilities for tree planting, Lucy and the team received another call from Professor Meridian.

"We have a serious problem on our hands, Locators. A volcano has erupted on the Galápagos Islands."

Lucy gave her full attention to the professor as she explained the situation. After all, volcanoes had the power to totally change the surrounding habitat, and could also be dangerous.

"The giant tortoises that live in the area are in trouble," the professor explained. "If the lava flows through their habitat, it'll be hard for them to get away in time. Lucy, I need you and your team to head for the islands, assess the damage, and find a way to help the tortoises."

"We're on it," Lucy said, jumping into action.

Their plane took them from Rio de Janeiro to the small nation of Ecuador on the western coast of South America. Not everyone was thrilled with the plan, however.

"Most people don't fly *toward* an erupting volcano," Oliver said, eyes wide.

"This is important, Oliver. The giant tortoises are in danger."

Moe landed on Lucy's shoulder. "*SQUAWK!* Why don't the tortoises just swim away, huh?"

"They're tortoises, not turtles. And they don't swim very well. And they're extremely slow," Lucy answered.

They landed in Ecuador and made preparations to fly over the ocean to the Galápagos Islands in a small plane the professor had arranged for them. The islands only had two airports, and both of them were pretty small. Neither Lucy nor Oliver was familiar with the route, and the ocean had few landmarks to help them navigate.

"We need to know how far the Galápagos Islands are from the coast of Ecuador," Oliver said. "That way we can stock enough fuel and make sure we're on the right path." He wanted to be absolutely certain they didn't run out of fuel and crash again, like in the Amazon.

Lucy's map didn't exactly say how far the islands were from the coast, though, and they didn't have much time. Impatiently, Lucy looked around the airport runway, but there was nobody nearby she could ask for information. She was about to call Professor Meridian when she remembered: the scale bar.

The map's scale bar indicated the connection between distance on the map and distance in the real world. Her map's scale bar represented 300 miles on the map, even though it was only about an inch long in real life. But it was a lot more than just an inch to reach the Galápagos Islands, even on the map.

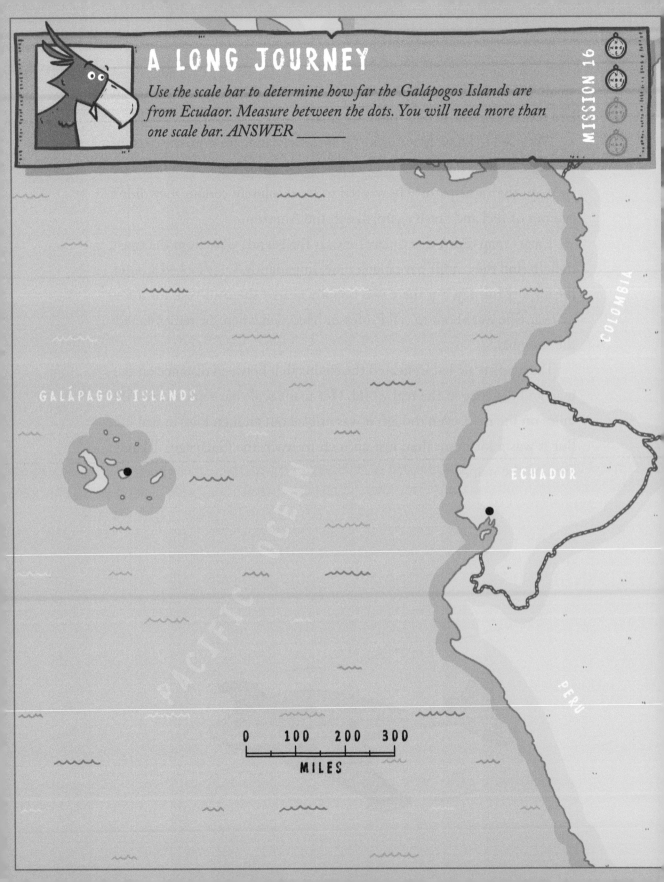

# A LONG JOURNEY

Use the scale bar to determine how far the Galápogos Islands are from Ecudaor. Measure between the dots. You will need more than one scale bar. ANSWER _____

COLOMBIA

GALÁPAGOS ISLANDS

ECUADOR

PACIFIC OCEAN

PERU

0    100    200    300

MILES

Lucy thought hard about the problem. The scale bar represented 300 miles, and they would need to fly the distance of about two or three scale bars to reach the islands. If she multiplied the number of scale bars by the distance of each scale bar, that meant the Galápagos Islands were between 600 and 900 miles away. Lucy estimated the exact number was close to 700.

"I guess now I can figure out how much fuel we'll need for the plane," Oliver said, shaking his head at the idea of setting the plane's autopilot to fly them into a volcano.

Soon they were off and over the vast, blue ocean. Lucy pressed her face to the window, stared down at the rippling waves, and waited.

"Too bad there's no in-flight movie," Moe said.

Eventually, small masses of land appeared on the distant horizon: the Galápagos Islands. Their mountainous volcanic peaks rose out of the flat ocean. From one of the peaks spewed a giant plume of smoke. "That must be the volcano that erupted," Lucy said. "Come on, Oliver, take us to it."

"OK, I am *definitely* putting my foot down. We are *not* flying straight to an erupting volcano," Oliver said, frowning.

Instead of landing near the volcano, they landed on one of the archipelago's two airports. The airport only had a few runways, but it was *just* big enough for the team's small airplane. As it turned out, the island that had the airport (Baltra Island) was not the same island where the volcano had erupted (Isabela Island).

Lucy lugged her equipment off the runway and through the airport. The Galápagos Islands looked like a weird combination of tropical paradise and barren desert. Some places had lush vegetation and beautiful

sandy beaches, while other places had rocky ridges with only a few shrubs. The airport was in one of the rocky areas. It was pretty busy due to the **eruption** but compared with Rio de Janeiro it seemed almost desolate.

"We'll need another way to reach the island," she said. "Oliver, do you know how to pilot a boat?"

Oliver shook his head. "Nope, not a single clue."

"Did somebody say they needed a boat?"

Lucy and Oliver turned and saw a woman in a khaki uniform, with a big, floppy hat and sunglasses. The woman had a huge smile, even though most of the other people in the airport were running around with worried looks. "Yes, we need a boat to Isabela Island," Lucy said. "Can you help us?"

"Sure can," the woman said. "Name's Maria. I'm a tour guide here on the Galápagos Islands. Right now, though, the tourists aren't exactly excited to get on my boat."

"Gee, I wonder why," Moe said.

"Maria, you have to help us," Lucy said. "Can you take us to the volcano?"

"I sure can," Maria said. "I'm always ready for adventure, and you guys seem like you've come prepared yourselves. Are you…scientists?"

"Students," Lucy corrected. "Although I'd love to be a scientist some-day. We're here to help the giant tortoises that are threatened due to the volcano."

"Perfect," Maria said. "Because the Galápagos Islands are so remote, you're one of the first people to arrive to help out. Come on, my boat's docked not far from here."

Maria's boat was usually used for tours, so it had comfy seats that helped win Moe over and an outlet to charge Oliver's laptop and phone, which helped win him over. They traveled west toward Isabela Island, the largest island in the archipelago. The bright-blue sky became darker and darker with ash as they neared the erupting volcano. Lucy and Oliver started to cough a lot.

When they got close to the island, Lucy saw the bright-orange lava that streamed down one side of the volcano. "We'll need to find someplace safe to land," Maria said, looking around. "The question is where."

Where, indeed? The lava was flowing down to the ocean. Lucy was ready to save the tortoises, but she wasn't crazy enough to try and land in molten rock. Not to mention, even if they docked somewhere that didn't have any lava at that moment, there was no guarantee lava wouldn't flow there soon. But at this distance, it wasn't clear which areas were safe. If only her map of the island showed where the lava was flowing…

She suddenly got an idea. "Eureka!" she said, using a word she'd heard the professor say.

"Oliver, when we went to the Andes Mountains and looked for chinchillas, Professor Meridian gave us a map that showed elevation. I need an elevation map, but for Isabela Island."

"That shouldn't be too hard to find," he said as he fiddled around on the tablet.

Soon, Lucy had a map of Isabela Island, with elevation indicated by number values. Her plan was simple: she would use the map to predict the direction lava was flowing (because lava, like any liquid, flowed from high elevations to low elevations).

Then she could find an area on the coast with a relatively high elevation, where it would be safer to dock. Areas farther from the lava would probably be safest, but they would also have to spend more time walking to reach the lava. Hopefully, she could find someplace close enough that also had a high elevation.

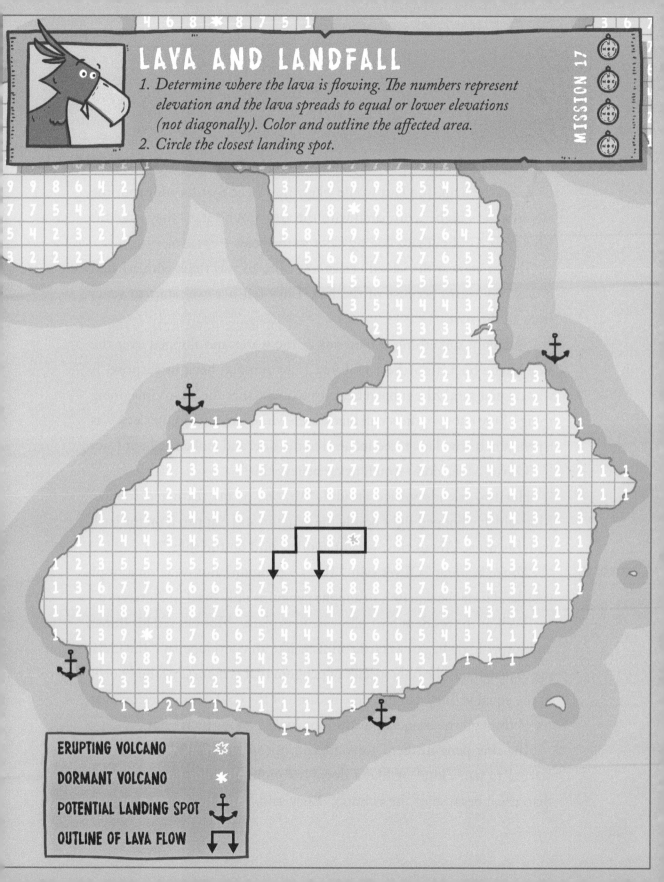

# LAVA AND LANDFALL

1. Determine where the lava is flowing. The numbers represent elevation and the lava spreads to equal or lower elevations (not diagonally). Color and outline the affected area.
2. Circle the closest landing spot.

ERUPTING VOLCANO

DORMANT VOLCANO

POTENTIAL LANDING SPOT

OUTLINE OF LAVA FLOW

A ha! Lucy found a spot that seemed good—the southernmost anchor on the map. The lava would likely flow near that location, but the elevation was higher compared with the area around it, so they wouldn't have to worry about lava oozing close to the boat.

They were near the island's coast now. The air was thick with ash and it was very warm because of the lava. Lucy felt her eyes start to water from all the soot.

Suddenly, something leaped out of the water and flopped over the side of the boat, right next to Lucy. Lucy jumped back in surprise. It was…a **penguin**? She rubbed her eyes to make sure she wasn't imagining things. Sure enough, the small black-and-white creature on the deck was a penguin. It stood up, tilted its head to the side, and looked right at Lucy.

"Oliver, Moe, look—you'll never believe this!"

Her two friends turned around. "Ah, one of my feathered friends," Moe said. He hopped right beside the penguin and clapped it on the back with his wing. "About time we got another bird on the ship."

"You're kidding," Oliver said. "That's a penguin? But we're on a tropical island near the equator. I thought penguins only lived in Antarctica."

"Well, as the resident bird, allow *me* to explain." Moe cleared his throat, and surprisingly began to rattle off facts like an encyclopedia. "The Galápagos penguin is the only species of penguin that is naturally found north of the equator. They can live here because of the cold ocean currents that travel through the islands. But this one looks like it's pretty hot."

The tiny penguin bent forward and opened its beak wide. It then started to pant, kind of like a dog. "It's probably a lot hotter outside than usual because of the volcano," Lucy said. "And the water nearby is probably pretty warm because of the lava flowing into it. It's not only the giant tortoise that has to worry."

"What's the matter, pal?" Moe said. "Too hot? This is nothing. You should feel the heat in the Amazon where I grew up. Now *that's* hot." Moe puffed out his chest. The penguin squawked in his face.

"We gotta help the poor little guy," Oliver said. "Wait, I have an idea."

He bent down to look under his seat. Lucy heard some shuffling and then Oliver appeared again. He was holding a big tan box: an ice chest.

"Maria, is it OK if we let the penguin take a little ice bath?"

Maria gave a thumbs-up. Oliver opened the ice chest, and he and Lucy pulled out all the water bottles and soft drinks, leaving only icy water. Then they helped the little penguin inside.

The penguin flapped his flippers and splashed the water around. He squawked happily in the cold water. Suddenly, another penguin hopped out of the ocean and onto the boat, followed by a third, and then a fourth. It seemed like they had come because they heard the call of their friend, and they all wanted inside the cool water.

With four penguins inside, the ice chest was a bit cramped, but the penguins didn't seem to mind—they were happy just to be out of the heat. They honked and squawked at Moe, who kept trying to "teach" the penguins the proper way to endure the heat.

Not long after, the boat reached the shore. "I'll stay here with the ship," Maria said. "You kids go and help the giant tortoises."

Lucy made sure the penguins were comfortable on the ship, and then she and her friends got going. Because they had docked near a higher elevation area, they had to climb some rocky cliffs to make it onto the island.

Lucy called Professor Meridian to tell her they had arrived. "Now that we're here, how can we help the tortoises?"

"The first thing you need to do is figure out how the volcano will change the island's environment," the professor said. "Surely you've noticed all the ash and rock under your feet, right?"

It was true. The ground was completely covered in sooty black dust and stone. "Is all this ash from the eruption?"

"Not just this eruption, but also thousands of eruptions in the past. There's not a patch of ground you're standing on that hasn't been altered by an eruption sometime in the past."

"Wow," Lucy said. "It looks like volcanic eruptions change the environment more than we thought."

"I guess it makes sense that the ash and lava from eruptions doesn't just disappear," Oliver said. "So it must become part of the ground."

"Lava? Part of the ground?" Moe said. "How's that even possible?"

"Lava cools off eventually," Professor Meridian said. "When it does, it turns hard, like rock. That's actually how the Galápagos Islands even exist—for millions of years, volcanoes kept erupting, until there was enough hardened lava to form an island."

"Wait," Oliver said. "That means we're walking on lava right now." He looked under his foot, as though he expected it to be on fire.

"Professor," Lucy said. "How do we find out how lava from *this* eruption will change the map?"

"That's simple. But it's time for you and your team to determine your next steps without my help. I know you can do it. Think you're up to the challenge, Locators?"

Lucy nodded, taking a big gulp. They'd be all on their own for this mission—with an erupting volcano! The professor ended the call, and then they really *were* alone.

Oliver and Moe stared with wide eyes, which only made her more nervous. They were relying on her to come up with a plan. She thought for a minute, brainstorming how they could help the tortoises. "OK…so first we need a map of the island to…map all the locations where you can find a giant tortoise. *Then* we can draw the lava flow on it to determine which tortoises are in danger."

"Great plan," Oliver said, nodding. He got to work on the tablet to bring up a map of the island as Lucy surveyed the environment. Even from afar, she could clearly see the lava—and, if she looked carefully, some of the giant tortoises. (They didn't call them "giant" tortoises for no reason.)

Her plan was going to work—it had to!

# LAVA FLOW AND TORTOISES

1. The lava flow may have changed! As before, color and outline the affected area. Remember, the lava will spread to equal or lower elevations (not diagonally).
2. Circle the tortoise populations in trouble.

# CHAPTER 20

"All done!" It had taken a while, but Lucy and the team managed to label the lava flow and determine which tortoises were in danger. Luckily, the tortoises had time to move out of the way of the lava. Tortoises might move slowly, but lava doesn't move much faster.

Lucy frowned, deep in thought. Based on the patterns where the team found tortoises, she had reached an unsettling conclusion.

"Oh no," she said. "It seems the lava went right through the biggest, most unbroken stretch of tortoise habitat." She remembered from the jaguar adventure in the Amazon that animal species could have difficulty navigating between smaller strips of habitat.

"What's the big deal?" Moe said. "You guys said yourselves that this whole island is cooled lava. Once it cools down, the tortoises can move right back, *no problemo*."

But Lucy wasn't so sure. "It's true, lava cools down eventually, but before it does that, it wipes out all the vegetation it touches." She flipped through her notebook. Giant tortoises were herbivores, which meant they depended on the local plant life for their meals. The plants would grow back eventually, but until then…

"The tortoises won't have anything to eat," she said. "Normally, this wouldn't be so bad. The tortoises are prepared to move to another part of the island if they have to, but things are changing."

"Changing? How?" Oliver asked.

"The natural habitat available to the tortoises has been reduced over time," Lucy said, reading from her notes. She looked around the island. There didn't seem to be any houses or buildings anywhere. "I wonder how… It's not like Rio de Janeiro. There's no city being built here."

Oliver chimed in. "I actually remember this from class—people can impact the environment in more ways than one. Over the years, sailors have brought animals such as rats, cats, and goats to the island, animal species that have never been here before. These new invasive species compete with native species such as tortoises and penguins."

Oliver, using his phone to search for more information, explained that goats and other introduced hoofed mammals ate a lot of the plants on the islands, while rats and other predators preyed on tortoise eggs. Because of that, the tortoise population on the Galápagos had declined incredibly.

"The point is, there's not much land left for the poor tortoises."

Lucy understood the problem better now. The tortoises could move somewhere else on the island after the volcano destroyed their habitat, but there just weren't enough good places to move *to*.

That meant she needed to find a good place for them. She asked Oliver to do a quick search on his phone to find out what food the Galápagos giant tortoises normally ate.

"Interesting. According to this, they like to chow on grasses, cacti, and fruits," Oliver said.

All they needed to do, then, was find a new place on the island with those kinds of foods and lead the tortoises to it.

"Oliver, Moe, come on. Time to explore."

She led her friends over the rocky beaches of Isabela Island. With the volcano still billowing smoke in the distance, they covered their faces with cloth to avoid breathing the volcanic ash. Everywhere, the giant Galápagos tortoises moved as fast as they could—which was not fast—to get away from the lava. Up close, they were even larger than Lucy expected. They were so large they were almost as big as Lucy and Oliver.

Soon, they reached a flat, grassy strip of land. It had been difficult to find because a lot of the island was dry and lacked dense plant life. But

## GALÁPAGOS TORTOISE

LIVES FOR MORE THAN 100 YEARS

CAN SURVIVE A YEAR WITHOUT FOOD AND WATER

ENDANGERED: MOST POPULATIONS RECOVERING

this area had shrubs and small trees surrounded by puddles of water. It seemed like a great place for the tortoises to go. Best of all, it wasn't in danger of being destroyed by the erupting volcano.

All that was left was to find some way to lead the tortoises to the new location. Moe and Oliver came up with a solution that involved tying some leaves to a stick and using it to lure the tortoises, which Lucy thought was impractical. As they argued over the best way to move the tortoises, however, they discovered that the tortoises had already started to move there themselves.

One by one, the giant tortoises lumbered up the rocky hills and joined Lucy and the team on the grassy meadow. Three, four, five… Lucy counted the tortoises as they gathered around the puddles and lapped at the water, or bit into the leaves on a tree branch. Soon, more than 10 of the massive creatures had arrived.

"What's going on?" Oliver said. "We went through all that work to find this place for them, and they knew about it already?"

"According to my notes, giant tortoises can live for over 100 years," Lucy said. "I guess they've explored a lot of this island and know all the best places to go already. Amazing! This is fantastic news."

She called the professor to report the situation.

"Well, well," the professor said. "What a fortunate turn. And good job, team. The tortoises are lucky they didn't stumble onto a grazing ground for goats. It might have been tough for them to find enough food to eat."

"Is there anything else we can do for the tortoises?" Lucy asked.

The professor thought deeply. "Hmm. Well, there is one thing… Do you see that mountain behind you?" She pointed and Lucy looked over her shoulder.

"Yeah, that's a dormant volcano, isn't it?" Lucy said.

"Astute as always. Now, take a look at that volcano and predict what might happen if it erupted. We were unprepared this time, and if not for good fortune, those tortoises might have been in trouble. Next time, however…"

"…We should prepare for an eruption beforehand," Lucy said. "We're on it!"

# PLANNING FOR ANOTHER

1. *The shaded area is the path of destruction from the first eruption. Color and outline the area that would be at risk from a lava flow from the other volcano. Follow the same elevation rules as before.*
2. *Circle all the safe tortoise populations.*

# CHAPTER 21

"Based on this map, it looks like a large number of tortoises would be affected if the other volcano erupts," Oliver said. "There won't be enough habitat for them all."

"*SQUAWK*," Moe said. "So what you're saying is, the turtles will go hungry if this volcano goes boom."

"They're tortoises, not turtles," Lucy said. "But this is not good news. Do we just have to hope the other volcano doesn't erupt? It could happen at any time."

"These are excellent deductions, my students." The professor was busy banging on a keyboard. "I'm typing your findings right now. The local authorities are trying their best to protect the tortoises, so they'll find this information quite helpful."

"But what can the authorities do?" Lucy said. "It's not like they can stop the eruption."

"They can do other things," the professor said. "If there's not enough habitat to support all the tortoises, they can airlift some of them to zoos and feed them until it's safe to send them back to the islands."

Lucy tried to imagine what it would look like to "airlift" a tortoise. She imagined them strapping the giant tortoise to a helicopter and flying away with it. It seemed silly, but if that was what it took to protect the tortoises, then she supposed it had to be done.

It wasn't her favorite ending—she wished there was a better way to help the tortoises in case of another eruption, but for now it would do. The volcano crisis was averted and the tortoises were safe. And she had led her team without the professor's help for the first time.

Lucy would have liked to stay on the islands longer and learn about

more of the unique species that called the islands home, but the volcano wouldn't allow that…and their adventure was drawing to a close. Soon, they needed to return home and start school again. Lucy, Oliver, and Moe said goodbye to the giant tortoises and returned to Maria's boat.

Now that the lava had cooled somewhat, they also had to release their penguin friends. "Bon voyage," Oliver said as he snapped a quick picture and then helped the little penguins out of the ice box and into the water. They squawked happily as they swam through the ocean, frolicking and playing with one another.

"This has been a real adventure," Lucy said, smiling as the boat sailed away from the island. "We crash-landed in the Amazon, climbed a mountain in the Andes, explored a jungle right next to Rio de Janeiro… and saw a volcano erupt in the Galápagos! Being a Locator definitely isn't for the faint of heart."

"You know," Oliver said. "All things considered, it was a pretty good trip. I learned a lot. And I feel a lot more confident as a Locator, too. I can't wait to make a map showing where we went to present to the class."

"*SQUAWK*," Moe said. "I just can't wait to be home sweet home."

Lucy laughed. But what Oliver said did make her think. With everything she'd learned on this expedition, maybe she ought to share some of her knowledge with her friends and fellow Locators. If more people knew about the challenges facing animals around the world, then they'd be a step closer to saving those animals from extinction. The job of a Locator was never finished.

The boat sailed away and the island grew smaller and smaller in the distance. Lucy could not wait for the next adventure…wherever it might be.

| A | B | C | D | E | F | G | H | I | J | K | L | M |
|---|---|---|---|---|---|---|---|---|---|---|---|---|
| 4 | 18 | 14 | 8 | 22 | 1 | 17 | 24 | 12 | 11 | 19 | 5 | 15 |

| N | O | P | Q | R | S | T | U | V | W | X | Y | Z |
|---|---|---|---|---|---|---|---|---|---|---|---|---|
| 9 | 3 | 13 | 20 | 10 | 21 | 7 | 25 | 23 | 2 | 26 | 16 | 6 |

12  9  23  4  21  12  23  22     21  13  22  14  12  22  21

*An organism that is not native to a particular area*

22  14  25  4  8  3  10

*A country in western South America with the capital Quito*

4  10  14  24  12  13  22  5  4  17  3

*A group of islands*

5  4  23  4

*Hot, melted rock that erupts from a volcano*

22  10  25  13  7  12  3  9

*When hot materials from the earth's interior are thrown out of a volcano*

24  22  10  18  12  23  3  10  22

*An animal that only feeds on plants*

# ANSWER THE QUESTIONS TO GET YOUR LOCATOR MEMBER ID.

1. *What is the last number of the year you were born?*

2. *In Mission 02, how many squares are between the crash site and the camp if the most efficient route is taken? Include the Camp and Crash squares.*

3. *Pick a number between 0 and 99. Write it as a two-digit number (for example, 7 becomes 07).*

4. *Have you been to South America? If yes, write 1. If not yet, write 2.*

5. *What exercise was the hardest? Write it as a two-digit number.*

6. *In Mission 15, how many hexagons did you think trees could be planted in (count the number of Xs you marked). Write the answer even if you were wrong (if more than 9, your number is 9)!*

7. *What was your favorite mission? Again, write it as a two-digit number.*

## LOCATOR MEMBER ID

*Your very own ID. We can't wait to see how you change the world!*

# ACTIVITY SOLUTIONS

## MISSION 01

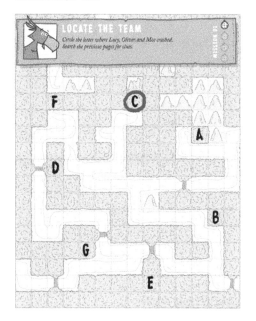

## MISSION 02

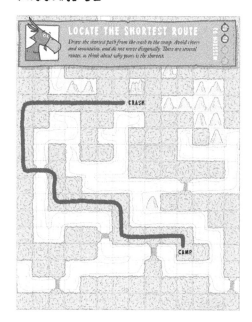

## MISSION 03

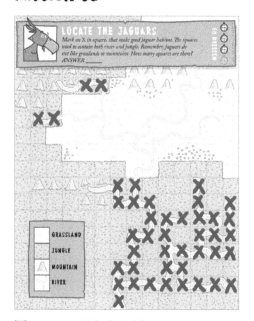

## MISSION 04

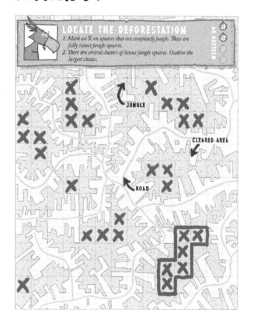

There are 43 habitable squares.

## MISSION 05

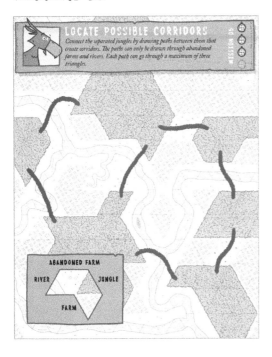

## CROSSWORD

**Across:**

4. Deforestation

8. Conservationist

9. Aerial imagery

10. Endangered species

**Down:**

1. Corridor

2. Meridian

3. Biome

5. Basin

6. Navigate

7. Leaching

## MISSION 06

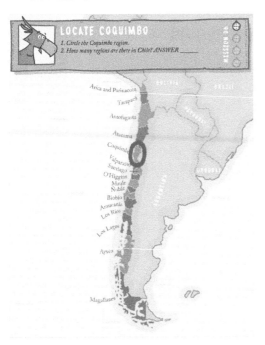

## MISSION 07

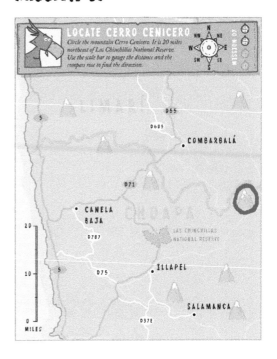

There are 16 regions.

# MISSION 08

LOCATE THE ALPINE BIOME

*Circle the alpine biome. Remember what Ranger Hernandez said, and look at the vegetation and terrain to determine the correct elevation.*

# MISSION 09

DESTINATION: SUMMIT

*Draw a path up the mountain that navigates the team from the base to the mountain's summit.*

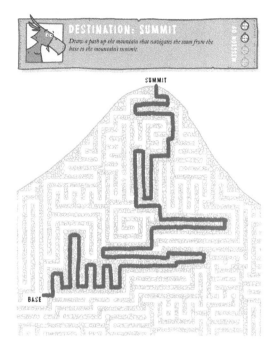

# MISSION 10

FIND A NEW PATH

*Wow, that was a close one! An avalanche has changed the terrain. Draw a new path for the team from the base to the mountain's summit.*

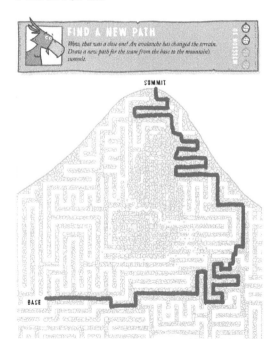

# MISSION 11

LOCATE CHINCHILLA HABITAT

*Connect the dots with the same values to create contours. Do not cross the lines. You will have three continuous lines (the 2000s, 3000s, and 4000s).*

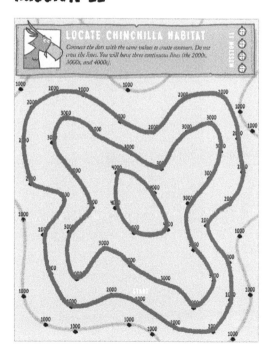

# WORD SEARCH

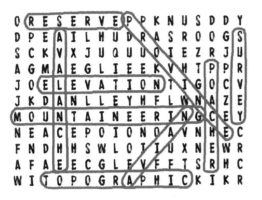

## MISSION 12

Land

Roads

Water

Cities

## MISSION 13

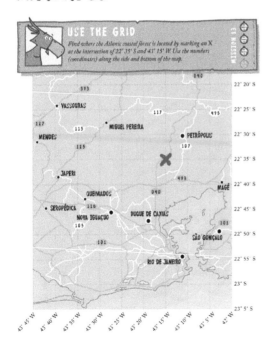

USE THE GRID

Find where the Atlantic coastal forest is located by marking an X at the intersection of 22° 35' S and 43° 15' W. Use the numbers (coordinates) along the side and bottom of the map.

## MISSION 14

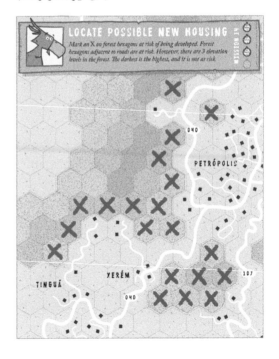

LOCATE POSSIBLE NEW HOUSING

Mark an X on forest hexagons at risk of being developed. Forest hexagons adjacent to roads are at risk. However, there are 3 elevation levels in the forest. The darkest is the highest, and it is not at risk.

# MISSION 15

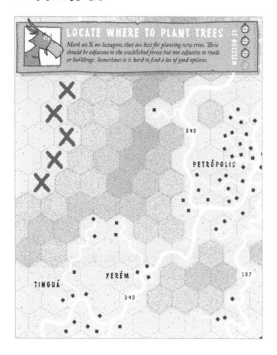

# WORD SCRAMBLE

Cartographer

Observation

Coordinates

Physical map

Absolute

Political map

Relative

Ecoregion

# MISSION 16

725 miles (Between 700 and 750 miles)

# MISSION 17

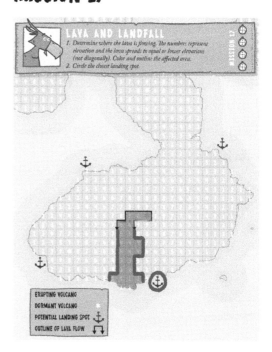

# MISSION 18

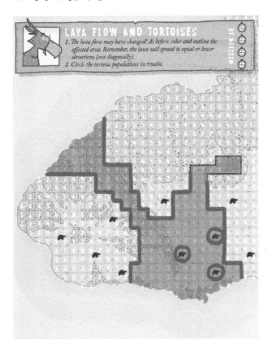

# MISSION 19

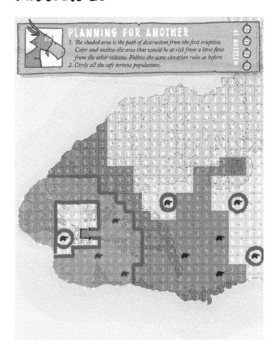

# CRYPTOGRAM

Invasive species

Ecuador

Archipelago

Lava

Eruption

Herbivore

# GLOSSARY

| | |
|---|---|
| absolute | Referring to the location of a place based on a fixed point on earth |
| aerial imagery | Photographs taken from an aircraft or other flying object that show the earth's surface or features |
| Amazon | A moist, broadleaf tropical rain forest |
| archipelago | A group of islands |
| avalanche | The sudden rush of a large amount of snow, ice, or rocks down a mountain |
| avian | Of or relating to birds |
| basin | A large area of land drained by a river |
| biome | An area that can be classified according to the plants and animals that live in it |
| Brazil | A country in eastern South America |
| caiman | A large reptile that is related to the crocodile and alligator. Caimans live in tropical areas of North and South America |
| cardinal direction | One of the following compass directions on the earth's surface: north, south, east, or west |
| cartographer | A person who draws or makes maps |
| Chile | A country in southern South America |

| | |
|---|---|
| chinchilla | A small mammal from the mountains of South America. Chinchillas are rodents closely related to guinea pigs. They have very soft fur and live in tunnels called burrows |
| coastal forest | Areas along the coast that are sheltered from the ocean |
| compass | An instrument for showing direction. A typical compass has a moving magnetic needle that points north |
| conservationist | A person who acts for the protection and preservation of the environment and wildlife |
| coordinates | A pair of numbers that identify a point on a map |
| corridor | An area of habitat connecting wildlife populations that are separated by human activities or structures |
| deforestation | The act or process of cutting down the trees of a forest |
| ecoregion | An area of land or water containing geographically distinct species, natural communities, and environmental conditions |
| Ecuador | A country in western South America on the Pacific coast. Quito is the capital of Ecuador |
| elevation | The height to which something rises or is raised, or its height above sea level or ground level |

| | |
|---|---|
| endangered species | A species of plant or animal that is in danger of becoming extinct |
| eruption | When hot rocks and gases from the earth's interior are thrown out of a volcano |
| expedition | A journey taken for a reason, or a group taking such a trip |
| GIS | An acronym for Geographic Information System, a system for gathering and organizing data so that it can be viewed on a map |
| herbivore | An animal that only feeds on plants |
| invasive species | A plant or animal that is not native to a particular area |
| lava | Hot, melted rock that erupts from a volcano |
| leaching | The process of nutrients being removed from soil |
| livestock | Animals raised or kept on a farm or ranch, such as cattle, horses, or sheep |
| llama | An animal closely related to the camel. Llamas are mammals that live in the mountains of South America |
| meridian | Half of an imaginary great circle on the earth's surface that passes through the North and South Poles |
| mountaineering | The sport of climbing to high points in mountainous regions |

| | |
|---|---|
| navigate | Plan and direct the route of travel, especially by using instruments or maps |
| observation | An act of watching someone or something carefully to gain information |
| penguin | A large water bird with webbed feet that lives in colder regions of the Southern Hemisphere. Penguins do not fly but use their wings like flippers for swimming |
| physical map | A map that shows physical features such as mountains, rivers, and lakes |
| poacher | One who illegally hunts on another's property |
| political map | A map that shows government boundaries for countries, states, and towns |
| province | A geographic division of a country |
| rain forest | A dense evergreen forest, mostly found in tropical areas, that receives a large amount of rain all year long |
| relative | Referring to the position of a place or entity based on its location with respect to other locations |
| reserve | Area of land that is protected and managed in order to preserve the habitat and flora |
| scale | A map element used to graphically represent distances on a map |

| | |
|---|---|
| scale bar | A line typically marked as a ruler in units proportional to a map's scale |
| sloth | A mammal that spends its entire life in trees, using its long claws to hang upside down. They move very slowly and are related to armadillos and anteaters |
| survey | To examine carefully |
| tamarin | A small monkey that lives in the forests of South America |
| topographic | A type of map that uses contour lines to show the shape of the earth's surface |
| tortoise | A turtle that lives on land |
| volcano | An opening in the earth's crust through which melted rock, ash, and gases are forced out |

## KYLE BAUER AUTHOR

Kyle Bauer is a product engineer on the Learn ArcGIS team at Esri, where he writes GIS tutorials based on real-world scenarios. His goal is to teach GIS in a way that is understandable to people without advanced technical knowledge of ArcGIS or other GIS software.

## COLLEEN CONNER CONCEPT

Colleen Conner has served 17 years as a corporate librarian at Esri, where she has devoted herself to building what is now one of the world's largest physical and virtual collections of maps and GIS-focused material. She champions the development of early spatial-thinking skills and recognizes the need for children's educational materials.

## WESLEY JONES ILLUSTRATOR

Wesley Jones is a professional cartographer who has worked at Esri for over a decade. When he is not making maps, he is drawing, and has illustrated comics and several books. Wes enjoys sports and being outside, but he especially enjoys storytelling. According to his children, his claim to fame is his bedtime make-up stories.

## REST OF THE CREW

Edited by Alycia Tornetta
Designed by Victoria Roberts
Developmental work by Nathan Shephard